A Sixpenny Song

Also by Jennifer Johnston

The Captains and the Kings
The Gates
How Many Miles to Babylon?
Shadows on our Skin
The Old Jest
The Christmas Tree
The Railway Station Man
Fool's Sanctuary
The Invisible Worm
The Illusionist
Two Moons
The Gingerbread Woman
This is Not a Novel
Grace and Truth
Foolish Mortals
Truth or Fiction
Shadowstory
A Sixpenny Song

Jennifer Johnston

A Sixpenny Song

TINDER PRESS

First published in 2013 by Tinder Press
An imprint of HEADLINE PUBLISHING GROUP

I

Cataloguing in Publication Data is available from the British Library

ISBN 978 1 4722 0922 1

Typeset in Centaur by Avon DataSet Ltd, Bidford-on-Avon, Warwickshire

Printed and bound in Great Britain by Clays Ltd, St Ives plc

Headline's policy is to use papers that are natural, renewable and recyclable products and made from wood grown in sustainable forests. The logging and manufacturing processes are expected to conform to the environmental regulations of the country of origin.

HEADLINE PUBLISHING GROUP
An Hachette UK Company
338 Euston Road
London NW1 3BH

www.tinderpress.co.uk
www.headline.co.uk
www.hachette.co.uk

To all my relations who live in and around Glasthale,

centre of the world, with much love.

Sing a song of sixpence,
A pocket full of rye;
Four and twenty blackbirds baked in a pie.
When the pie was opened,
The birds began to sing;
Wasn't that a dainty dish to set before the king?

She hadn't really liked him very much, Dada (he preferred it if she called him Father; to him Dada was an untidy name for a man of his standing).

The king was in his counting house,
Counting out his money . . .

From the tip of his head, black hair slightly streaked with silver the last time she had seen him, which she would have to admit was ten years ago, to the toes of his highly polished shoes he looked immaculate, handsome, a man of class and wealth. Which, of course, he was. He liked things to go his way; his word was law, and always what he thought was the best for you.

'I only want what is best for you.'

How many times had she heard those unanswerable words?

And now he was dead. She wondered if he had ordered his death as he had ordered everything else in his life.

She hadn't been back here for over ten years.

She had been barely eighteen when she had left Dublin. She had just thrown some stuff in a suitcase and set off as so many others had done down the years and indeed still do for their various reasons. Her reason had been freedom, her destination London. From London it had appeared to her she could survey the world; she would be able to make decisions, her own decisions, not her father's. Dada had a scheme mapped out for her. He had wanted her to follow him into the money world. He wanted her to move with grace and confidence among the wheelers and dealers and eventually marry one of them and consolidate their assets, their two worlds. He had sent her to school in England a couple of years after her mother had died, when she was barely twelve years old and too young to fight her corner. 'I only want what is best for you,' he had said, when he had dropped the bombshell. 'Your mother and I have only ever wanted the best.'

How can you fight against someone who only wants the best for you?

You can't. You have to run. Oh, yes, in the end you have to run.

Luckily for her she had friends in London, thanks to Dada's choice of school for her; she had a little money in her bank account, thanks also to her father's being a rich man and giving her a decent allowance, which he docked when he realised she had gone. He thought he could frighten her into returning to Dublin, but he was wrong; Jude and Annie had been the two failures in his life. They had both escaped him.

It didn't take Annie long to get a job in a bookshop

just off the King's Road; it must have been the smallest bookshop in the world, but was undoubtedly the best. The three young men who worked there were all called John, or rather John, Johnny and Sean; this made Annie laugh. She bought herself a bicycle and every day, hail, rain or snow, she would pedal from her tiny flat in Notting Hill through the park to the Albert Hall, downhill past those imposing museums to South Kensington and then on to the King's Road. It was harder work going home, but it was still an enjoyable part of her day.

She became a Londoner; it's an easy thing to do, just a question of smiling, keeping your equilibrium, being polite, and smiling some more, and after a while they no longer notice that you are not one of them. There are myriad different sorts, bumping fairly gently up against each other, scraping, joking, fighting, loving, hating, the whole of life's gamut, in fact. She became absorbed into it.

There was another bookshop just round the corner from her flat, owned by a man from Belfast. He also owned a dog that used to sit by the door of the shop and smile at customers as they went in. Silly things like that made her feel good; made her laugh. She felt good a lot of the time in London; even the dust and the east wind and the petrol fumes couldn't diminish her feeling of joy at being free. Even the voice that from time to time spoke in her head. 'This is not home.' It would speak quite clearly, with a slight Dublin accent. 'You silly girl, you must go home before you forget, before you are forgotten.' She would laugh, of course; in those days voices in the head were to be laughed at. Now they have become more sombre; now they have in them intimations of mortality. Great words, those, with a fine rhythm to them. She had always loved words, the way they roll from your mouth, sonorous, or fly like birds, little flitting birds or frightening black crows. She always used to ask Jude the meanings of words she had never heard before.

'What does persevere mean, Mummy? What is an ogre? What does it mean in your music book when it says *allegro ma non troppo*? What is a pedagogue?' Once, she remembered whining at her, 'There are so many words, will I ever know them all? Will I, Mummy, will I?'

Jude had laughed, and tousled her daughter's hair with her fingers. 'I expect you'll know every word you need to know. The unexpected ones that you've never met before and probably never will again you will find in the dictionary. You must always be sure you have a dictionary, because that is an enormously important book. And a thesaurus. You will need one of those too.'

'What's a thesaurus?'

Jude had had enough. She reached for her glass. 'Run along, darling. Go and find Nanny.'

The maid was in the garden,
Hanging out the clothes,
When down came a blackbird and pecked off her nose.

And here she was in the middle of Dublin Airport with that silly song whirling in her head.

It was always a child singing in her head. A young fresh voice. A sweet voice. Her voice?

She didn't think she had sung as well as that. In fact she was pretty sure she hadn't.

She stopped walking and shook her head, to dislodge the voice. She must not lose reality, not here. Dublin Airport was not a place for fantasising.

'Keep your wits about you,' Johnny had said, as he had dropped her at Heathrow, just this morning.

She had only been in the shop for about fifteen minutes when he had called to her. 'Annie. Telephone.'

She had been dusting top-shelf books with a feather duster. 'Who?' She made her way to the front of the shop and he handed her the receiver.

'Your mother.'

'My mother,' she said sharply to him, 'has been dead for almost twenty years. So that's pretty unlikely.'

'Ah,' said Johnny. 'Sympathies and apologies. An impostor then. You may not want to speak to an impostor.'

'Hello, this is Annie Ross. Who is speaking, please?'

'Darling Annie. This is Miriam, your . . . yes . . .'

'Oh yes, Miriam. How are you?' She grimaced at Johnny and rolled her eyes towards the ceiling.

'Dear child, I have some very sad news for you. Your father . . .'

'My father?'

'Yes. He, well, he's dead. He died. Quite suddenly. He just stood up from the table after breakfast and dropped dead. Like a stone. The doctor said he had a massive heart attack. Massive. About three hours ago.'

There was a very long silence. There was a sound like a sob from Miriam's end.

Annie sighed. 'Poor Dada.'

'He wouldn't have felt a thing. He went down, as I said, like a stone.'

'Poor Dada. I'll . . . I'll come . . . I'll . . .'

'Dead. Will you come? Could you? I know you haven't been near him for years.'

'I'll be over this evening.'

'I knew you'd come. I knew you were a good girl at heart.'

'I'll see you this evening.'

'Someone will be there to pick you up.'

'No. That's OK. I can get a cab. I don't know what plane I'll be on and I won't need a bed. I'll stay in a hotel.'

'Annie . . .'

'I'd rather. I'll see you this evening.'

She put down the receiver and sat thinking about Dada. I couldn't sleep in the same house as his dead body, she thought. No.

Mrs number two wife, better known to the world as Miriam, had served him well; she knew the value and importance of money, she knew what to spend and where to spend it. I am rich, her charming smile seemed to say, please come and enjoy my richness for a while. Yes, she served him well, and had, no doubt, been well rewarded; she had her little pad now in Monte Carlo, where everyone was rich, and she would wait there to see what the wind would blow in her direction.

I have never wanted to be her friend, so I don't want to sleep in the same house as her live body.

Johnny had put his hand on her shoulder. 'Come on, Annie,' he said. 'I have the car outside. I'll drive you home to get your stuff and then out to the airport. Come on, quick. We don't want you blubbing all over the shop.'

She didn't blub.

Her head felt as if it were full of stones, each one rubbing against the next one, creating little aches behind her eyes.

'I didn't like him,' she said to Johnny as she got into his car.

'That's OK by me. The world is full of people who don't like their fathers or mothers. Or come to that their brothers or sisters. No need for guilt or apologies. Something will make you cry, though. You will be surprised by tears. They will happen.' He began to hum a tuneless song and they drove to the airport without speaking.

* * *

It wasn't until she saw the house, standing resplendent on what looked like its own private hill and backed by the low mountains, Kilmashogue, the Hell Fire Club, the dark shadowy Pine Forest, and the sad ruin directly behind it, the name of which escaped her at that moment – it had been burned in the troubles and only the elegant shell remained to remind people of those days of painful violence – that she began to cry, unstoppable warm tears, bursting from her eyes. She scrabbled in her bag but couldn't find a Kleenex and was just about to use the sleeve of her coat when she felt the taxi driver pressing a bundle of tissues into her hand.

'Thanks.'

It hadn't been the sight of her father's house that had caused her to cry, but the fact that she was not able to remember the name of the ruin.

Nanny and I used to go up there at the end of August, each with two chip baskets which we would fill with fat berries, and we never minded the scrapes from the brambles or the stains on our clothes, fingers and faces. She remembered that well, and the wonderful taste of the berries, fresh from the hedges as they burst in your mouth.

She blew her nose. 'I'm sorry.' What the hell was that house called? Did it matter? Not a jot.

'Are you all right? Do you want me to stop for a few minutes?'

'No thanks. I'm OK now. Thank you. You've been so kind.'

'*De nada,* lady, *de nada.*'

That made her smile.

He swung the car right down the lane between the two cottages, deep and dark under the trees interlacing overhead, over the little humpbacked bridge and up the hill and there she was, home. She warned her eyes not to weep again, and looked instead at all of Dublin stretched beneath her, miles of rooftops and spires, factory chimneys and the odd sparkle of the sun on windows, all swathed in blue haze. I had forgotten, she thought. Mummy always said remember, but I hadn't remembered this.

The hall door opened behind her and she heard the

sound of feet descending the granite steps. She sat tight where she was, staring out at Dublin. The door of the taxi opened and a hand was laid on her shoulder.

'Annie. Annie, my dear.'

'Hello, Miriam. I'm terribly sorry . . .' She stopped. 'I'm terribly . . .'

Miriam gave her a scented kiss on the side of her face.

'That's all right, my pet. You don't have to say anything. Come in.'

She was dressed in a smart charcoal grey suit, almost but not quite black, and round her neck she had tied a pink silk scarf that trembled gently in the wind.

Annie got out of the car and followed Miriam up the steps. Once they were in the hall and the door was shut they stood and looked at each other.

'It's the same as it's always been,' said Miriam at last. 'He had such good taste, your poor dear father.'

'Yes,' said Annie.

'There'll be tea,' said Miriam. 'I just wondered if you'd like to see him first.'

'No . . . I'm sorry . . . no. I couldn't. I mean . . . no. Thank you.'

'You're sure?'

'Oh yes. Certain. I just want to remember him the way . . .'

'Quite,' said Miriam. She sounded a little put out.

'I hope you understand. I have a picture of him in my head. I don't want it replaced.'

'Sit down. I'll just go and tell them to bring tea.'

Dada looked up from the paper as she moved into the room.

'Ah, Annie.' Genial smile. He was sitting in an armchair by the fire. 'Sit, sit, dear child. Over here near the fire.' Obediently she moved towards the fireplace, towards him, his legs crossed negligently, the paper drooping from his fingers. She was twelve. She wondered as she crossed the room whether someone cut his nails for him, they looked so proper and trimmed. He let the paper drop to the floor.

'Everything OK?'

'Yes, Dada.'

'Not lonely?'

She shook her head.

'That's good. It doesn't do to be lonely. We might go to the pictures one evening. A Friday or Saturday. If there's anything on that you'd like to see.'

'That'd be nice.'

'You could bring a friend.'

'Thank you.'

'Something suitable, of course. In the meantime, join me for dinner tonight. How about that? Quarter to eight in here. There's someone coming who I'd like you to meet. Her name is Miriam Talbot. Wear something tidy. She's a nice lady, you'll like her.'

'Yes, Dada.'

'Good girl. Quarter to eight. What are you doing this afternoon?'

'I'm going swimming with Helen and Sophie. I'm meeting them in Sandycove.'

'How do you get to Sandycove from here?'

'Bike.'

A tense little frown appeared on his forehead. 'You will be careful, won't you? It's a long way. Uphill all the way back.'

'I do it all the time.'

'Oh . . . I didn't realise. Harry could always take you in the car.'

'No, thank you. I enjoy riding the bike. I can whizz down. Coming back is a bit slower, but I can manage OK. I'll go and have tea with Helen. We do it most Saturdays in the summer.'

'You won't be late for dinner, will you?'

She stared at him and didn't say anything.

'There's just one other thing . . . umm . . . something that your mother and I discussed for a long time.' He clasped his hands in front of him as if he were about to pray. 'Yes. The time has come, I think, what with one thing and another, for you to go to school in England.'

'I don't want to go to school in England.'

'None the less, it is the moment. It is arranged. And

your mother, if she were still here, would agree. I know that for a fact.'

'I want to stay here. I don't want to go to boarding school anywhere. I want to stay here. I want to stay at home.'

She felt a hot rush of tears coming into her eyes. She didn't want to cry. Crying was useless, she knew that, especially with him. He didn't care about tears; they merely made him angry. She pinched the top of her nose between two fingers. The room became splinters, her father splintered, the big armchair, Mummy's grand piano, the windows looking out over the garden, all splinters.

'I want to stay here.' Foolish repetition. 'I don't know anyone in England.'

'Your mother and I decided on a school for you a long time ago.' He coughed. 'Yes. Indeed we did. I have been over to see it. It's very beautiful, and it has an excellent academic record. All excellent. I have spoken to parents. And the sports . . . You will make friends, my dear. You are a very friendly person. In no time at all. I am sure of that. The head is a very lovely lady. Altogether . . . your mother . . .'

'Do shut up, Dada. We both know perfectly well that Mummy would never have wanted me to go to school in England.'

'There is going to be no argument about this. You're going in September and that's all there is to it. You must trust me to know what is best for you. Taking all the circumstances into consideration. Now run away and swim with your friends. Are you sure you don't want Harry to take you in the car?'

She shook her head and stood up.

'Quarter to eight,' he said. 'We must have more little chats.'

No arguing with the king, she had known that. He never wore a crown, but you knew that he was a king, without a doubt.

Where else, she wondered, would he be waiting for her? The hall, on the stairs, the dining room? In his counting house, as Jude called his very private study?

'I don't think I can bear it.' She said the words out loud.

'Bear what?' Miriam came back into the room. 'Tea will be along in a moment.'

'What is the difference between a ghost and a memory?'

'Is this a riddle? I'm not much good at riddles.'

'It's just a question.'

'Well, this house isn't haunted, if that's any help. But you should know that. You lived here for eighteen years.'

'Will you go on living here?'

Miriam looked at her, startled. 'Good heavens no. It's not my house. It's your house. I'm just a visitor here really. Your guest.'

Annie gave a little gulp of laughter. 'You're joking.'

'Of course I'm not joking. Why would I joke about such a thing?' The door opened and a girl came in with the tea tray. 'Thank you. Just leave it on the table.' They watched in silence until the girl had left the room once more. 'Will I pour? Why would I joke?'

'I just thought . . .'

'Your father has left you the house. I imagine you can do what you want with it. Mr O'Brien will—'

'Who is Mr O'Brien?'

'Your father's lawyer. He will tell you all tomorrow. After the funeral.'

'The funeral is tomorrow?'

'Yes.'

'In England they keep you hanging around for weeks.'

Miriam handed Annie a cup of tea, then poured her own and took it across the room to a chair by the fire. She sat. She looked most elegant, Annie thought.

'Mr O'Brien will explain all. You see, your father, apart from a few little legacies here and there, left most of his money to me. He knew that I would be able to handle it.'

'And I wouldn't?'

'Well . . .'

'Well what?'

'I just think he thought that you wouldn't appreciate it. He always said that you didn't understand the importance of money. So . . . he left you the house. It must be worth quite a lot. He actually said you were quite like your mother . . . feckless was the word he used.'

'Thank you.'

'I don't think he meant anything hurtful by it, just not caring. Your mother didn't care about money, did she?'

Annie didn't answer.

'Money needs to be cared for, nurtured. I know how to deal with it. Your father was great with money; he was like a gardener, he made it grow. He watered it, fed it. Anyway, in the end he decided to leave you the house. He wondered if he should leave you money . . . you know, tied up so that you couldn't do anything foolish with it, a certain sum each year, you know, income, but then he thought in the end that the house would be best and you could sell it or whatever. Whatever.' She took a sip of her tea. 'Cake?'

'No thanks.'

'I shall go to Monaco. I have a little flat in Monte.'

She leaned forward and took a piece of cake. She looked at it for a long time as if she were regretting having taken it, then took a large bite. 'Nyum, so good, do have a piece.'

Annie shook her head. She really wanted to go, not just to her hotel, but all the way back to Notting Hill.

'Do you know Monte? It's a heavenly place.'

'No. I've never been there.'

'Next door to paradise. And the prince is a sweetie. You should go and visit sometime. It's full of interesting people. I don't have a spare room, otherwise . . .'

'Don't worry, I—'

'You really should try that cake.'

'No thanks. Is there anything you want me to do? If not, I'll—'

'Oh, must you? No. Nothing. Everything is under control. If you'll be here at half past ten tomorrow morning you can come in the car with me. That would be the best thing to do. Don't you think? Have you friends you'd like to ask to lunch? You can see Mr O'Brien when lunch is finished. I'm sure all your father's old friends will be delighted to see you again, after so long.'

'So.' Annie got to her feet. 'If there isn't anything I can do, I'll go. I'll be here at ten thirty. Thank you so much for the tea.'

She left the room; she left Mrs number two wife sitting by the fire with a rim of chocolate cream on her top lip.

She told Johnny about it all when she arrived back in the shop the following Monday, and he laughed. He then stopped laughing and said he was sorry.

'Why sorry?' she asked. 'It probably was quite funny. Disagreeable but funny.'

'We all thought that you'd arrive back here bloody rich and snooty and you say he hasn't left you any money. That's quite funny.'

'I suppose it is. I've got this lovely house, though.'

'What good is a lovely house if you don't have enough money to live in it?'

'Quite.'

* * *

Give her all the time she needs to gather herself together without exhausting herself. She can take what she wants, except for Mother's piano, which I'm sure would be a terrible encumbrance to her. I am asking you as my lawyer to do this for me. I have no great wish to see her ever again, and I'm sure that she would feel the same about me. When she has gone I shall be selling the house and buying something much smaller and more suitable nearer to town. If you would let me know when she will be going I will come over to Dublin and with your help sort out my life . . . hopefully I will remain over there.

She wrote this in a letter to Mr O'Brien a couple of weeks after she had returned to London and the next day she told John, Johnny and Sean that she would be leaving soon to go back home and open a bookshop.

'You poor mad girl,' one of them said.

Another laughed. 'Why not just stay here?'

'Anyway, bookshops will be a thing of the past soon.'

'We love you, baby. Stay with us.'

'It's the bloody internet. Everyone will be buying books on the internet.'

'It's ghastly, but it's true. Worse still, they'll stop buying books altogether. They'll start reading off the screen.'

'Soon books will be museum pieces. People will forget how to turn pages.'

'In spite of all that doom and gloom we wish you luck, ducky.'

Mad little conversations like this kept flipping around her. Her friends gave farewell parties for her; several young men, who obviously thought she was rich, asked her to marry them. Of course she laughed and said no to all of them. It was spring. And London is always good in the spring and Annie began to worry about the plan she had made. Perhaps she shouldn't move back to Ireland. Perhaps her home was here now. Perhaps it was her fate to be an exile for ever. A cheerful exile, not one of those ones who cries and moans. No, she would be a cheerful exile, happy to be in London, happy to be a

Londoner. Happy to have no voices in her head.

So when Mr O'Brien telephoned to say that Miriam had gone and the coast was clear for her to return, it was on the tip of her tongue to tell him she had changed her mind and would he put the house in the hands of agents – and would he send her the money when it was all done and dusted.

'I will never go over there again,' she said inside her head. 'I will stay with John, Johnny and Sean for ever. I will buy myself a sweet little house in Notting Hill, with window boxes and a bright red door, and settle myself there for life.'

'Remember.'

Quite clearly she heard Jude's voice in her ear. Just the one word. 'Remember.' She always used to say it. 'Remember.'

It was her departing word; she would then leave the room, or the garden, or walk slowly up the stairs, leaving the word trailing behind her, scarf-like, undulating in the breeze.

'Remember.'

She felt her mother's breath brush her cheek.

'I will be over in about a week,' she said to the solicitor. Her heart lifted as she spoke the words. 'I'll see you then.'

'Remember.'

The following Tuesday she had been leaving Mr O'Brien's rather palatial office in Merrion Square when he called her back. She stood with her hand on the polished brass doorknob and waited to hear what he had to say.

'You mentioned the fact that you wanted to open a bookshop. That is correct?'

'Yes, quite correct.'

'Have you a notion where you want this shop to be?'

'No notion at all. Somewhere obviously that people live. Live and shop and have children and read. A centre of population.'

'Of course. It might be worth your while having a look in Glasthule village. I live quite close and I noticed the other day that there is a shop there for sale. It's not very big.'

'Size doesn't matter.'

'Well, you should have a look.' He paused for a moment. 'You know, my dear, I am on your side. I told your father . . . well, I told your father . . . but she . . . there you go. We will get the best possible price for the house and set you up with your bookshop. I am your father's executor and I will see you right, young woman. I will buy books from your shop, indeed I will. I have long wanted my own personal bookshop. Adjacent. Certainly. I will drive you crazy with my adjacency. All hours of the day and night I will be there asking for abstruse books in abstruse languages. My dream come true.'

Annie laughed. 'I'm sure I'll learn how to deal with bothersome customers quite quickly.'

'Well, go and have a look at it anyway. Goodbye, my dear. *A tout à l'heure.*'

Nice man to have on your side, she thought as she walked back to her car.

* * *

The road from Dun Laoghaire to Dalkey meanders, past the People's Park on the left and the railway and the horrible place for parking cars. Glimpses of the sea flicker on the left as it wanders past the huge church and the houses holding consulting rooms for doctors and dentists, past a garage and a florist's shop, and round the corner into Glasthule village, which is not really a village any longer. Not so many years ago it was one with all the right shops: baker, greengrocer, butcher, fishmonger, a newspaper shop and a chemist, a cobbler, three pubs and a cinema; almost everything you might have wanted could be found there at that long bend in the road. Now it has changed, not physically – the road still bends, the shops cluster on each side of the curve and apart from the cinema, which is now a small and ugly block of flats, everything looks the same: reddish brick, somewhat Victorian, nothing to write home about – but when you look more closely at them you will find that the fishmonger is now an expensive restaurant, which only does lunch, and there are three other restaurants, two expensive shoe shops, three dress shops, a wine bar, a coffee shop, two off-licences, an antique dealer and a very green vegetable shop. Two of the pubs have gone and the chemist and the cobbler still remain.

No one here knows that I exist yet. How could they be expected to? I have never lived here, only bicycled through on my way to swim in Sandycove, with my two friends. Children we were, before my uprooting.

She stood on the edge of the pavement and thought and stared across the road at the shop between the wine bar and the antique shop. A large notice jutted out from between the first-floor windows.

For Sale.

She wondered if you could catch a glimpse of the sea from the back windows. That would be good, even just a glimpse. A shining glimpse.

The lights at the crossroads changed to red and she ran across the road, slipping past the stationary cars and trucks.

The shop window was stylishly decorated with expensive children's clothes: Liberty print silk dresses with smocking and tiny puffed sleeves, tweed jackets for boys, with slim cut trousers. Oh my God, she thought, no wonder they're selling up. No self-respecting child would be seen dead in those clothes nowadays. Long white knee socks and patent leather shoes. They wear boots and skirts that barely cover their bums, baggy jumpers and ripped jeans. For heaven's sake!

She took a pen and a notebook from her bag and wrote down the name of the estate agent, the telephone number and address. Two girls inside the shop stared at her; she smiled at them and they turned away quickly. She put the notebook back in her bag. If she could see the sea from one of the top windows she would definitely buy it. I will be able to lie in bed and look at the waves, she thought. I will be able to see the lighthouses flashing before I go to sleep. I will be able to see that hideous car ferry rushing across the bay, ripping open the water as it goes. I will be able to see the lifeboat and at weekends the yachts racing, propelled by the wind, dancing across the wrinkled sea.

She walked towards the car. *Sing a song of sixpence.* The song was still in her head. *A pocket full of rye. Four and twenty blackbirds baked in a pie.*

Only they weren't, were they? No, no no. Because . . . *when the pie was opened the birds began to sing,* so baked they were not.

A relic of childhood? *Wasn't that a dainty dish to set before the king?*

Here I am in Glasthule, she thought. I have no past here, no voices, no sad or angry memories, just the whirr of bicycle wheels and a dim recollection of the shop where we used to buy four penny sliders and then the long drag, uphill all the way home. Stiff legs and her face burning with the sun. The sun always shone when you were a child.

As if to reprimand her for such a thought, a drop of rain burst on the side of her face. Within moments the drops became a furious outpouring, bouncing up from the pavements and the roofs of the cars; women were struggling with the hoods of buggies and people were jostling each other for shelter in shop doorways. She searched through her pockets for the key of the car.

The king was in his counting house. Yes, always. It never rained in the counting house, which had every comfort, fresh flowers and the background music of coins rattling into a money box.

She found the key and pressed it; the lights flashed on her car on the other side of the road and she dashed through the rain and the traffic and slid into the driving seat and mopped at her face.

He never wore a crown, but he was definitely a king. If she closed her eyes she could see him, black-haired, immaculately dressed, silk shirts and suits from Armani.

Counting out his money.

Someone banged on the window of the car.

'Are you moving or just sitting there? You have me blocked in.' An angry woman holding a newspaper over her head pushed her face against the window.

'Oh. I am so sorry. I didn't realise . . . so sorry.'

She put the key in the ignition and moved the car out into the traffic. She waved cheerfully at the woman as she drove off. The woman did not wave back.

I like this neck of the woods, she thought: I like its mixture of rich and poor, its fine Victorian houses and its cottages, the gardens burdened with flowers, the inescapable smell of the sea. I could stay here for ever. I could call it home. Perhaps the rooms over the children's clothes shop could become home.

Home.

She had been in danger of calling Notting Hill home.

She turned left. There was disburdening to do.

Yes. His home; his counting house. The voices. *The maid was in the garden, Hanging out the clothes . . .*

'Why?' she had asked Mummy once. 'Why the maid? What did the maid do wrong?'

They had been sitting in the garden. Mummy sat under a parasol; she had delicate skin. The sun was torture to her. Her glass was at hand on the round wooden table next to her.

'Why did that horrid blackbird peck off her nose? Why do the wrong people get punished? It's so unfair.'

Mummy had taken a drink, just a little sip.

'That's the way the world is, Annie. It's pretty unfair. Remember. Don't ask me whys and wherefores. No point in doing that, precious one. I don't know the answers either.'

'I can play that song on the piano.'

'Can you indeed? Then run in, there's a good girl, throw the window open and play it for me.'

As she ran up the steps Mummy called after her, '*Fortissimo,* my darling, play it *fortissimo*. Beginning to end, as loud as you can manage.'

She had played it once and then because she had made a couple of mistakes she played it again. And she had sung the words in a strong, clear voice. Perfect. *Fortissimo,* just as Jude had asked, and she had finished off with two magnificent chords. Dominant, tonic. Pom. Pom.

She will be pleased, Annie had thought as she ran to the window to take her bow. But no one was there. The parasol lay on the table. Jude had disappeared.

'Just like that.' She clicked her fingers. 'Gone.' The rain streamed on across the windscreen. Disburdening.

To her intense surprise she remembered the way, although all the fields had been built over; houses, flats, garages, small industrial buildings now covered the open space there once had been. From time to time a landmark poked its head towards her and she felt confident once more: a church that she remembered; a yellow pub; an old factory, now crumbled by a river bank, those left of the blue letters on the wall that had once been brighter than the sky now washed by the rain, almost white, illegible. A sign pointed to a golf club. She wondered if Dada had had a hand in that. He had played golf; he had liked golf clubs, they were a healthy way to keep nature in check, keep it manicured. She had always thought that he would love to have seen Ireland as a conglomeration of golf clubs and race courses, seaside ones, mountain ones, flat middle of the island ones, all serviced by hotels and cities, offering entertainment and shopping for the world's rich golfers and racegoers. She laughed at the thought and then saw the house sitting on its little hill, waiting for her. The rain had stopped and there was a streak of gold across the sky; maybe the sun was trying to come out in a rather half-hearted sort of way.

The house was protected from development, not just by its age but also by its large garden, which rolled comfortably down the hill to the trees at the bottom – oak, chestnut, sycamore – and the stream which bubbled and bounced through the rocks and had never seemed to lack water, even in the hottest and driest summer.

She turned down the lane between the two cottages, into the darkness and over the humpbacked bridge, then all of a sudden she was at the bottom of the steps on the neat gravel half-moon. Water dripped merrily from the roof and the trees, and the gravel shone as if it had been polished. As she began to search through her bag for the house key she heard the sound of feet scrunching across the gravel. She opened the car door.

'Can I help you?' A tall man was standing staring down at her. His voice was polite.

'I don't think so, thank you.' Her fingers found the key in the bottom of the bag. She got out of the car. He wasn't much taller than she was, and his hair was long and curly, much of it tucked into a knitted red cap.

'There's no one in.'

She waved the key at him. 'I know. But I shall be in in a moment. Who are you, anyway?'

'What does it matter who I am? This is private property.'

'My private property.'

He raised his eyebrows, but didn't say a word.

She marched up the steps to the front door. She was now staring down at him, in a commanding position, one might say. He didn't look very happy; he didn't look as though he believed her.

'My name is Ross, Annie Ross. This is . . . well . . . umm . . . my house. There's someone coming to look it over. And I'm here now, so if you'd, well, not interfere. Please. Do you have a name?' She opened the door and waited on the threshold for him to speak.

'Kevin.'

'Kevin.' The name meant nothing to her. 'What are you doing here?'

'I do odd jobs. I keep the garden clean. I mend the gutters. That sort of thing.'

I wonder if I am paying your wages, she thought, or whether Mrs number two wife is? 'I'll see you later. If you have to speak to the man who's coming, just tell him that I'm here. Tell him to ring the bell. Just be polite.'

He scowled at her. She went into the house and closed the door.

The house smelled clean and polished, no dust or dead flies. Dada had loved flowers, everywhere, great tall stems of pampas grass in the hall, branches of rhododendrons and azaleas, wax-like camellias, massed daffodils in the spring, roses, red, yellow, white, pink, and then at the very end of summer and through the autumn pots of golden, copper and white chrysanthemums. Always flowers. Mummy disliked this over-abundance; she used to rush upstairs with her handkerchief to her nose. 'The house smells like a bloody florist's shop.' Then she would slam the door of her room and that would be that.

'Why, anyway?' Annie had asked her once. 'Do you not like flowers?'

'I do, darling, I do, but not too many flowers. Except, of course, in the garden. If you put too many in the house it seems as if you're trying to hide the smell of death. Creepy.' She always had her glass at hand, and her hand had always shaken when she stretched it out to pick up the glass. 'The smell of death.'

Then there had been the day she had run up the stairs and opened the door of Mummy's room; Jude had been standing by the window staring down at the garden below.

'I am dying, Egypt, dying.' There was a long silence; neither of them moved or said a word. Then Mummy spoke again. 'Remember. Just remember, there's a good girl . . . and keep Shakespeare near at hand; he's got a quote for every eventuality. The Bible has too, but I think Shakespeare is better.' She laughed, a rather sad little laugh. 'Remember.'

'What am I to remember, Mummy?'

'You used to dance. When you were about five.

With me. We used to bounce around the room. See me dance the polka. One two three hop. Do you remember that?'

'Not really.'

'Well try. That's the sort of thing to remember. Happiness. Of course there were other happy moments too, but dancing is . . .' Her voice faded away.

'What?'

'Dada used to be a wonderful dancer. We . . . well anyway it doesn't matter now. That's all over.'

'No it's not. Nothing's over till you're dead.'

'Did they teach you that at school?' A sarcastic note in her voice.

'No. They don't teach you anything like that at school.'

There was another short silence.

'I'd better go.'

'Yes. You go. Vamoose, be gone, fly, disappear, escape. Yes, escape.'

She had left the room, closing the door quietly behind her. She stood for a moment on the landing, listening to her mother's voice repeating the word.

'Escape, escape, escape.'

Now, as she stood in the hall, the word seemed alive, swooping and darting like a swallow. It tumbled down the stairs and echoed off the pale yellow walls, spoken in her mother's deep, almost breathless voice; it came across the many years and then stopped as suddenly as it had begun and the house was silent once more.

She threw her bag on to a chair and went into the drawing room. Those must have been the last words my mother said to me, she thought. Escape. Or had she been merely talking to herself? Had she forgotten the presence of her child as she had issued those commands?

The drawing room was empty of furniture, apart from the grand piano which looked forlorn without even its piano stool; it was ebony and had cost Dada a small fortune, or so he had told them the day it had arrived. It had *Steinway* written in gold letters on the inside of the lid and she had not been allowed to play it unless her hands were clean.

Maybe I could sell it with the house; des. res. with view and Steinway.

Am I funny, she wondered. Well, I think so anyway. Sometimes.

She heard the wheels of a car outside, scrunching the gravel.

What the hell was the man's name? Something Scottish. Mac . . .

The car door slammed. She walked across the hall. Let him be constructive, imaginative, positive. Hamilton? Campbell?

She opened the door. He looked confused; his hand had been raised to ring the bell.

'I'm sorry. I gave you a fright. I've only just arrived myself.'

'No, no. James Fraser. How do you do?'

'Come in, Mr Fraser. We're going to have to find some chairs to sit on. My . . . ah . . . stepmother seems to have emptied the house of its furniture. The only thing left in the drawing room is the piano.'

'Tut,' he said.

She didn't think that was either constructive, imaginative or positive. 'Come and see.' She led him across the hall. He took a notebook and pen out of his pocket as he followed her.

'Hmm,' he said as he looked round the empty sun-splashed room.

'She never told me that she was taking the furniture,' Annie said. She wondered if her voice sounded fractious. 'Of course it was hers to take and it doesn't really make any difference, does it? I mean to say.'

He wrote something in his notebook and smiled at her, a nice reassuring smile. 'I wouldn't let it worry you.'

'I'm sure you'd like a cup of coffee. I'll go and make coffee and you can wander round without me trailing behind you. You can just give me a shout if there's anything you want to know.'

'How kind. A cup of coffee would be very nice. I presume . . .'

'Nowhere is out of bounds. The kitchen is the other side of the hall, down two steps and turn left. Take your time. Please don't feel you have to rush. I'll wait there for you. Maybe she hasn't taken the chairs from the kitchen.'

She nodded at him, in what she hoped was a friendly way, and turned and walked quickly out of the room.

To her intense surprise the kitchen was fully furnished and on the long table was a tray set with cups and milk and sugar and a plate of biscuits. Beside the tray was a coffee pot and a large jar of coffee, while on the edge of one of the hobs of the Aga the lid of the kettle rattled. It's like the bloody *Marie Celeste,* she thought.

Then she remembered that Cocteau film, *La Belle et le Bête,* and the bodiless hands holding candles. Inviting you deeper and deeper into mystery. *There's no mystery here, only memories, my head's memories, and the sooner I get rid of them the better.* She spooned some coffee into the coffee pot.

My dream will come true, thanks to Dada.

Thanks to Dada.

She had never thought she would hear herself saying those words.

She sat down by the table in the kitchen and thought about Dada; she wondered if he had ever been in the kitchen, had ever sat, maybe, in the chair she was sitting in now. Probably not; there was a line drawn in his mind between men's and women's duties. He was not one of those pouffy types who liked kitchens, who enjoyed rustling up an omelette or twirling a salad in a bowl. As far as he was concerned food was definitely woman's stuff. But he loved flowers, rejoiced in a vase beautifully arranged, would clap his hands and call for Mrs Cooke to congratulate her on her artistry.

'Bravo, bravo, Mrs Cooke, you've done it again,' he would say to her when she came into the room. And she would beam and chuckle.

Bonhomie and charm. He had them in abundance, like the icing on an expensive cake.

'I remember meeting your father once,' people would say to her. 'Such a charming man.' And she would smile and nod. What else can you do?

She listened carefully to the sounds made by Mr Fraser as he wandered in and out of lonely empty rooms.

Mr Fraser, relieved of the burden of his client, opened and closed doors, checked cupboards, examined sash cords. He even, purely for his own amusement, played a few notes on the piano. They sang out clear and tuneful and he shut the lid down again with a certain embarrassment. The dining room had also been stripped of furniture, apart from a large sideboard on the wall opposite the windows, and the room appeared lonely and a little depressed. Through the windows you could see Dublin away below, smoking and glinting in the sun which shone from behind the house, and then beyond the city the deep blue line of the sea. Mr Fraser wrote things in his notebook, he shook the radiators, he turned on the taps in the washbasins and flushed each loo. After about three quarters of an hour he descended to the kitchen with a happy smile on his face. The delicious smell of coffee came up the stairs to welcome him. Good, he thought to himself, this is a good ticket.

'Well?'

He sat down. 'It's a lovely house. In very good nick.'

'My father was very particular. He liked everything to be just so. I hope we'll get a good price for it.' She poured out a cup of coffee and pushed it towards him. 'Milk? Sugar? I have plans, you see, for the money. I intend to start a bookshop. I've even seen the place I want to buy.' She couldn't think why she was telling him this.

He stirred some sugar into his coffee. 'No problems about probate or anything like that?'

'Oh, no. Nothing like that. It's all quite clear and straightforward.'

'Good, good. You never can tell. Sometimes awful shocks and bothers appear. It all has to be sorted out before you can sell the house.'

'It will be all right. I know that for absolutely sure.'

'It's a good substantial house. How much land attached?'

'About ten acres, just down to the other side of the bridge. My father dammed the stream to make a swimming pool. That's an amenity these days, isn't it?

Then there's the tennis court and a vegetable garden. Ten acres, I think.'

'I'll go and have a wander round when I've finished my coffee.' He took a long drink from his cup. 'I'll send out a photographer tomorrow. I think I can safely say that we will be very happy to sell this property for you.'

'Quickly, I hope.'

He gave a little smile and nodded his head.

She decided that she quite liked him; she wondered if he had any bookshops up his sleeve.

After Mr Fraser had gone, after she had watched his car bumping down the hill and over the bridge, she went back to the kitchen and poured herself another cup of coffee and sat once more at the kitchen table. Outside someone was clipping a hedge with electric clippers. She presumed it was Kevin at work. The coffee was cold. Distasteful. She pushed it away.

Dada used to leave the house each morning at eight thirty, driven by Mr Cooke. Annie would stand at the nursery window and wave at his car as it went down the avenue and over the bridge. The bridge was humpbacked and the moment the car crossed it, it was gone, out of sight until Mr Cooke drove it back some time later, took off his flat cap and dark suit and put on his gardener's clothes and began what he thought of as his real job. Mummy always preferred to drive herself. She would throw her bag on to the passenger seat and take off, waving out of the window and tootling her horn merrily all the way down to the gate. Annie always used to wonder where she went filled with such gaiety. Dada put a stop to that, however; one evening he was home before her. He opened the front door and was there standing waiting for her as she came up the steps. Annie was at the top of the stairs, about to run down and hug her mother, but something stopped her and instead she leaned over the banisters and listened to her father's voice. Cold it was, cold as the perishing sea.

'May I ask where you have been?'

'In town. Dublin, not London, Paris or Rome. Just Dublin. I had lunch with some pals.'

'It's long after six.'

'So?' She pushed past him into the hall. 'Do you want me to give you their names and addresses? My palsy walsies?'

'You know I don't like Annie coming home to an empty house.'

Mummy had laughed. 'That is of course silly. There's Mrs Cooke. Mr Cooke. Harry, who does nothing but follow Mr Cooke around all day.' She was ticking each name off on her fingers. 'Nanny and two girls. That makes six. What do you mean, an empty house?'

'You know perfectly well what I mean.'

She took off her coat and threw it on a chair. It was her fur coat, so it must have been winter. She walked towards the drawing room.

'Where do you think you're going? I'm speaking to you.'

'You can speak to me in here. I'm getting myself a drink.'

'No. You shall not. You will go to your room and

get ready for dinner. Maybe you don't remember that we have guests coming?'

She stopped walking and looked him up and down. 'I am getting myself a drink.'

He stepped sideways, between her and the door. 'No. You are going up to your room and doing what I say. And when you come down you will be sober and you will behave like a civilised human being and not a drunken . . .'

She turned away and walked across the hall to the stairs and up past Annie, leaving behind her a whiff of whiskey and Chanel No. 5.

'What is the matter with Mummy?' She had gone down the stairs and crossed the hall towards Dada. He was standing just where Mummy had left him, tapping his foot angrily on the floor.

'Oh . . . ah . . . Annie. I didn't know you were there. She's . . . ah . . . ill. A bit ill. Yes. She's not well.' He frowned. 'Not well.' He coughed.

'Will the doctor make her better?'

'Yes. Well . . . she doesn't want to get better. That's

the problem . . . the difficulty. You have to want to get better.'

'Suppose—'

'Run along to Nanny.'

'She's with Mummy. She's almost always with Mummy.'

'Haven't you got homework to do?'

'It was only reading. Easy peasy. I am best in the class at reading.'

He turned and went into the drawing room and closed the door.

Annie picked up the dirty coffee cups and carried them over to the sink. She rinsed them and left them upside down on the draining board. Someone else would deal with them, some immaculate person, paid for either by Mrs number two wife or by her. I suppose I will know one day, she thought, what ghostlike creature keeps the place so immaculate. She had a momentary picture of Mrs number two wife sitting by a swimming pool in Monte Carlo, surrounded by handsome ageing men, all rich, all charming, all on the lookout for the right rich woman, someone called Miriam.

What age was I when I left, went to seek my own modest fortune? Eighteen. Yes. I had to go. He had my future mapped out for me.

I must leave this house. It makes me remember too much. I don't really like that.

'Remember.'

As she heard the voice being whispered she wondered if Jude had said that to Dada also. Probably not. You didn't tell Dada what to do.

There must be some happy memories here. Of course there were; her childhood bedroom had a tall press in it with ducks painted on it, red, blue and yellow ducks who quacked at each other and smiled joyfully under neat sailing clouds. She had loved those ducks. At night, as her eyes drifted into sleep, they spoke to her in a secret language that only she could understand, and in the darkness they lost their colour. She would wake early in the morning hoping to see them flying in through the open window and taking their places on the press, but they were always too quick and too cunning for her. She must have been very young to get such pleasure from these cheerful paintings, because when she was about ten she came home from school one day to find that they were gone, ducks and clouds and press and all, and there was a Georgian chest of drawers in their place. Charming, no doubt, valuable, no doubt, but not her friendly ducks.

'Your father thought it was more suitable, now that you're into double figures. Not a kiddlywink any longer.'

'But my ducks, where have they gone? Will they be happy?'

'Don't be silly, darling. Mrs Cooke's niece has just had a baby and Dada gave it to them. They were delighted.'

'Nobody asked me.'

Mummy put one finger on the side of her nose and rolled her eyes to heaven. 'Tut tut,' she said, and left the room. She looked young then, and walked lightly; the drink had not yet crippled her with its weight.

She must have spoken to Dada the moment he came

home from his office because he came up to the nursery to see Annie, something he seldom did.

'Darling girl.' He put his arms round her and hugged her tight. 'I have annoyed you.' He threw himself into an armchair by the fire and pulled her down on to his knee. 'I am filled with remorse. Here you are nearly grown up and I do a thing like that. So silly of me. Of course I should have asked you if it was all right. I do hope you like the new chest I bought you, but if you don't I will get you another. We might even be able to manage that you could come to the auction with me. That would be fun, wouldn't it? A really grown-up thing to do. What do you say, girl? Come, give your stupid father a kiss.'

She had kissed him. She remembered how much she had loved him at that moment. The warmth from that moment touched her now as she sat in the kitchen.

Strange thing was, no one ever mentioned the duck press again, or the new chest of drawers, neither Mummy nor Dada, not a single soul. He never took her to an auction, but equally he never again tried to get rid of anything that she might have considered to be hers.

Or had he?

What about her life? Her freedom?

Wasn't that why I left this lovely house, she wondered, preferring to go to London rather than staying here and learning the secrets of the money markets, the buying and selling of money, the glory of balance sheets, the joy of watching your assets grow. The counting-house life. That was what he had decided was for me. Determined was a better word, she thought now. He was a determined man.

They had been having dinner alone, she and her father. It was before the official arrival on the scene of Mrs number two; he was wining and dining her all right, but seldom at the house yet. It was a beautiful evening. The sky behind the house was opal, the sun almost gone, and sparks of orange shone in the windows of the city below them. It was almost the end of August; Annie had left the English school and was going to Trinity in the autumn. She felt grown up. He was in a good humour.

'What day of the week is it?' He was peeling a pear as he spoke, the skin ringleting down on to his plate.

'Wednesday.'

'Mmm. I think you can start at the office on Monday.'

Annie had laughed.

'Why do you laugh?'

'What makes you say a thing like that? Why would I start in the office?'

'I have thought long and hard about this, Annie. You must learn about business and it seems to me the best thing you can do is come into the office right away. Start off at the bottom . . . a gofer, running messages, doing the post, keeping your ear to the ground.'

She had held up her hand. 'Shh. Shh, Dada. I don't want to work in your office, or anyone's office. Thank you very much all the same. I don't want to run messages or do the post. I'm going to Trinity. You know that.

You never objected to that. In October. I'm going to read English. I'm going to find out about all those books I know nothing about. That's what I want to do. That's what I'm going to do.'

'If you'd been a boy—'

'I'm not a boy.'

'If, as I was saying, you'd been a boy, you would have gone into the business the moment you were finished with school. As I did. There was none of this university nonsense for me. My father set me to work straight away. He was right. There's no time to be lost was what he said to me. No time for chasing degrees, for messing about with the unmotivated. There is no place in the world as it is today for the unmotivated.'

'Dada . . .' She had tried to stop him, but the words tumbled from his mouth like a waterfall. On and on they tumbled and splashed around her, and all she could do was sit and listen to him telling her the plans he had for the rest of her life. The words went in one ear and out the other.

'You start on Monday,' he said finally, and there was

silence. 'Miss O'Reilly will be expecting you at nine o'clock sharp.'

There was more silence.

'Thank you, Dada,' she said. She reached out and took a pear from the fruit bowl and peeled it and began to eat it.

'Good. That's settled then.' He pushed back his chair and began to get up.

'Well actually, no.'

He sat down again. 'What do you mean, no?'

'No. Just that.'

'Is Monday too soon for you? We could make a slight adjustment.'

'I want to have a bookshop.'

He laughed. 'There's no money in books.'

'It's what I want, though, ever since I was thirteen. I've thought about it. I want to go to college and learn about books, as much about books as I can cram into my head, and then open a shop. A small bookshop. I want to sell beautiful books, books with history, books that people cannot resist buying. They will take them down from the shelves with care and love. I want—'

'There's no money at all in small. You will learn that in time. Yes. Monday—'

'I want to know every book in my shop. I don't want to be selling products, I want to be selling a way of looking at the world. A way of—'

'Business sense. Know-how. Fiscal imagination. The pure joy of making money, watching it grow. You should look at it as if it were a garden. A well-tended garden, nothing crude, wonderful, colourful growth . . .'

'*The maid was in the garden hanging out—*'

'What's that? A non sequitur. You could become like your mother. Her conversation was filled with non sequiturs.'

'I was too young to notice.'

'You can take it from me.'

'She used to say "remember". That's all I can recall. Little short sentences and then "remember". She loved books.'

'I do not wish to talk about your mother.' Then he pushed back his chair again and stood up. 'Monday morning,' he said and left the room. He didn't look back; he didn't see Annie shaking her head.

She had sat in the dining room for a long time after he had gone and wondered about a lot of things. She remembered his hands, his thumbs plaited together, hovering in front of her face. *Down came a blackbird and PECKED off her nose.* Peck, his hands would swoop towards her and lo and behold there was her nose held tight between his fingers. She had hated that. She had been frightened, and he had been amused by her fear. She had small memories of moments of love, but that was all. He always wanted to win, and he almost always did, even the smallest joust, with the youngest person around, which usually happened to be her.

Almost every Saturday he went racing; Mr Cooke, wearing his dark grey flat cap and his uniform jacket, would drive him off at twelve o'clock to meet his friends in time for a quick lunch before the first race at two o'clock. Leopardstown, the Curragh, Phoenix Park, and in the spring all the glorious point to points. He always returned in the evening looking pleased with himself, as if he had always won. He used to take a shining half-crown from his pocket and hand it to her. 'Make it grow,' he would say to her as he pressed the coin into her fist. But she would spend the money on comics: *Playbox, Dandy* and *Beano*. The money he gave her never grew; it never had time to grow.

Whenever she remembered Jude, fragility was the word that came into her head, a word like snapping twigs. It was not the right word for her. She had faded away. Each day she had seemed to become more transparent, each bedtime kiss more insubstantial, her voice fainter, leaving less and less echo in the air. Then she was gone – just gone. Annie had arrived home from school to be met by Nanny at the door, Nanny in tears, Nanny as she had never seen her before. She had thrown her arms round Annie and gasped through her tears, 'She's gone.' Just those words.

Annie had been startled by Nanny's tears. 'Who? Who's gone?'

'Your mummy. Your darling mummy. Gone.'

'Where's she gone, Nanny?' She was puzzled by

Nanny's gulping, by the rawness of her face. 'Nanny!'

'She's gone, the poor little thing, to God. She's . . .' She didn't like to use the word. 'She's . . .'

Dada's hand was on Annie's shoulder. 'That's all right, Josie.' He never called her Nanny. 'Off you go and have a cup of tea with Mrs Cooke. Annie will be all right with me.' He put both his arms round her and hugged her tight. 'She is Dada's little girl. Dada's pet. We will manage this together, won't we?'

Annie pushed him away. 'Where is Mummy? What has happened? I want to see Mummy.'

He took her arm. 'No. You come with me. In here, come. I'll tell you. Come with Dada.' He pulled her towards the drawing room and unwillingly she went with him. He closed the door behind them. 'Yes. Yes. My dear little girl. Your mummy's dead. She's passed away.'

'But Dada, how? I saw her before I went to school. She can't be dead. You're only pulling my leg. Aren't you?'

He shook his head.

'Aren't you, Dada?'

'No, Annie, no, I'm not. I'm really sorry, but your mother's dead. Nanny found her dead when she brought up her coffee for her. About eleven. Yes. Dead. She's dead.' He pulled a handkerchief from his pocket and blew his nose. 'Dead.'

She didn't know whether to believe him or not. Her brain seemed fractured by puzzlement.

'I saw her. She said "see you this afternoon". She wouldn't have said that if . . . Would she? She wasn't ill.'

She remembered her standing by the window of her room, and her voice, I am dying, Egypt, dying, and her sad laugh.

'You never told me she was ill. How can you die if you're not ill?'

'Sometimes death catches you unawares. No warning.' He blew his nose again and she began to cry. He pulled her to him. 'There, there,' he said. 'There, there. At least we know she will be happy now. We must be thankful for that.'

'I want to go and see her now.'

'No. No. You may not do that. Remember her as she was this morning.'

'Dada, please.'

'No, and I have said no also to the people upstairs, so there is no point in you sneaking off when my back is turned. Dead bodies are not healthy for children to gape at.'

'Dada . . .'

'You must do what I say.' Tears burst out from his eyes. 'I cannot bear it when people do not do what I say.'

'I will do what you say, Dada. I'm sorry. Please don't cry. Please.'

He pushed his handkerchief into a pocket and patted her shoulder.

'That's my girl. Sit down there now and I'll ring for tea.'

She didn't want tea, but she did what he had told her to do and watched him cross the room to the fireplace, where he pressed the bell. Then he walked to the window and stared out down the avenue.

'A quick cup will clear my head.' He spoke to himself rather than to her. 'Before they come.'

'Who will come, Dada?'

'It would be best if you were to pop up to your room. The people will come to take Mummy to the hospital.'

'Why do they have to take her to the hospital?'

'They must check to see why she died.'

'Why did she die? You said she wasn't ill. You have to tell me, Dada.'

'I don't know, darling. She just didn't seem to want to live.'

'Did she not like you?'

There was a very long pause.

'I don't know.'

She considered his answer.

'Mothers and fathers are supposed to like each other.' The door opened and one of the girls came in with the tea.

* * *

There was a knock on the kitchen door which made her jump from the past into the present. Her heart thudded. She couldn't think for a moment where she was.

'Yes. Hello. Come in.'

Kevin came in and carefully closed the door behind him. She wondered for a moment if he was going to attack her with the secateurs he was holding in his hand. Her heart thudded again.

'Yes. Hello.' She wondered if her voice sounded nervous. 'Erm, would you like a cup of coffee?'

'No thanks.'

'Tea?'

He stood staring at her. She wondered if he had heard her. Finally he shook his head.

'No tea. Thanks. No. Was I rude?' He shifted the secateurs from one hand to the other. 'I thought maybe that I was rude. So . . .'

She waited for him to finish, but he didn't; he just stood there staring.

'I don't think you meant to be rude. Why don't you sit down?'

He nodded. He moved across the room and pulled out a chair from the table and sat.

'I thought I should clear that up and if you thought I had been rude I would apologise.'

'No need, I do assure you. I was just caught by surprise.'

'Well that's all right then.' He pushed the secateurs into the pocket of his coat. 'Odd job man. That's my profession.'

'Are you sure you won't have a cup of tea?'

'No thanks. I bring my own. It's safer. You never know what people will give you. There's so much muck around. You don't remember me.'

'No. Oh, dear. Am I the rude one now? Should I remember you? It's so long since I've been here.'

'I remember your mother. She used to play the piano for us. You and me. I am of course quite a bit older than you. We would sit on the drawing room sofa and she would play and sing. My aunt lives on the other side of the hill and I used to come and visit her from time to time.'

'Miss Dundas?'

'That's the one.'

'I remember her. She visited Mummy quite a lot. I don't remember you, though.'

'I just trailed behind her. A shadow.'

'How is she?'

'Old. She hates that. I live in her yard. Sort of keep an eye on her. Do odd jobs around the place. See she comes to no harm.'

'Who pays you to come here? Me? Or . . . or . . . ?'

'She does. Until things are sorted out. She said she just wanted things kept tidy. I come over three days a week.'

'I suppose I should pay you from now on, until the place is sold. That would seem fairer, don't you think? It's really nothing to do with her any longer.'

'You're selling the place?'

'Yes.'

'Hmm.'

'It really isn't any of your business what I do with the damn house.'

'I suppose not. My aunt will be interested, though. Close neighbour and all that. She'll be upset that you're selling up.'

'Tell her I'll be over to see her in the next week or so. I'll just pop in one day.'

'She'd like that. She talks a lot about your mother. She painted a lovely portrait of her, rather Edwardian-looking, holding a big straw hat. You might like to see it.'

'I didn't know she painted.'

'Oh yes, she did indeed. She can't any more; that's one of the things that makes her angry. Her hands shake. It's hard to paint with shaking hands. Why do you sit in here? There are all those other lovely rooms. It seems odd that you should entertain your guests in the kitchen.'

'I haven't had any guests, just you and the house agent. Mrs number two wife . . . I mean Mrs Ross . . . took all the furniture.' She stood up. 'I think it's time you went now.'

'I didn't mean to upset you.'

'You haven't. I have to go. Please tell your aunt that I will be over to see her. And I will talk to my father's solicitor about paying you. Goodbye.' She stood and watched him as he got up and walked across the kitchen. At the door he stopped.

'Goodbye, Miss Ross. If there's any particular thing you want me to do . . .'

'No thanks, just keep on the way you are. Everything looks fine. I'm sure it will sell quickly.'

He nodded and left the room, leaving the door open behind him.

'By the way, my name is Annie,' she called after him. He didn't reply.

She gathered the coffee cups on to the tray and stood up. Then she was suddenly conscious of a slight sound behind her and turned. He was standing in the doorway staring at her.

'Yes?' Her voice sounded anxious. 'Yes?'

'There was just something I wanted to ask you.'

'Fire away.'

'I have always wondered . . . I hope you don't mind

me asking, but I've wondered for so long . . . did you know that your mother did away with herself?'

Annie groped for a chair and sat down.

'My mother . . . my . . . what did you say?'

He remained silent.

'Why did you ask me an idiotic question like that? My mother . . . my . . . never.'

'I'm sorry. I'm terribly sorry. I was told—'

'That was a lie you were told. My mother died. She never . . . My mother just died.'

'Jude.' He just said the one word and then he was gone.

She didn't even hear his steps on the passage floor. She thought for a moment that he had been a figment, just like the other figments that had been teasing her since she had come to Dublin, then she pulled herself together and thought about his words. His real words.

She didn't sleep that night. The moon shone on her face; she had always hated that. She felt as though the whiteness of its light pierced her eyelids, exposing her brain to too much brightness. Even with the window open the room seemed airless, full of objects that creaked and moaned; she fought with the pillows several times and the traffic droned inexorably outside in the street. At about four thirty she gave up the struggle, switched on the light and lay staring up at the ceiling until it seemed to be time to get up.

Miss Dundas. Foremost in her mind.

Yes.

She wondered if she would be able to find the house.

She wondered what would be a polite time to arrive.

She wondered if she would discover something that she didn't want to know.

She thought she might.

She wondered why he, the odd job man, had felt the need to ask her such a question.

Was it true, what he had implied?

Had her mother . . . ?

Had she . . . ?

Annie did not believe for one second that her mother had killed herself. Why would she? After all, didn't she have everything that she could have wanted? Annie heard Dada's voice.

'Everything that money can buy.'

How great that sounded, until, of course, you started to think about it; then it became perhaps ashes in the mouth.

She was drifting.

Was Mummy's mouth full of ashes?

Drifting.

She sang. The odd job man and Annie sat on the sofa and listened.

Her mouth was full of ashes.

Drifting.

* * *

It was raining, soft grey misty rain that embraced you and lay on your face and hair and on your shoulders. She turned in through the wrought-iron gate and bumped along the pitted, curling drive. The trees looked soft and grey too, their branches drooping, tired of winter, towards the ground.

It was a charming house, two storeys high, with long windows and a healthy wisteria trained up the front wall, with bright green curlicues just about to burst into flower.

As Annie opened the door of the car the hall door of the house opened and an old woman stood there, leaning on a stick. She lifted her left hand in greeting and smiled.

'Annie, my dear.'

She got out of the car and went towards her. 'Miss Dundas.'

'Kevin led me to believe that you might come. Don't slip, dear child. This gravel is fearfully slippy. It is so good of you to come and visit an old, old lady. What a day. What a day!'

They shook hands and Annie wondered whether to kiss the other woman or not. Miss Dundas drew her into the hall and shut the door behind them. It was a huge room with a big fire crackling at the far end, sending sparks spraying up the chimney as the logs were devoured.

Miss Dundas waved her stick towards the chairs that scattered the hall.

'We use the hall for sitting these days. I eat here and watch TV here. I would sleep here, but I prefer to go upstairs to bed. Old-fashioned, I know, but that's the way I am. I write letters here, I read books here. It makes life much easier when you are old to be a one room person. Do sit, my dear. I hoped you might come. It is so good to see a new face. Well, newish. It must be twelve years. No more like twenty. Time passes so fast. I can't remember when I saw you last. It wasn't long before your dear mother . . . oh, and by the way, I was really sorry to hear of your father's death. Please accept . . .' The words drifted to a halt.

'Thank you.' Annie sat down. Miss Dundas looked her up and down.

'You don't look like your mother. She was such a delicate-looking person. She looked as though she would blow away with a puff from the wind. I liked your mother; I missed her when she was gone. I painted her once. Rather good. I will show you when we've had coffee. It's in the drawing room.'

'Thank you, I'd like to see it.'

Miss Dundas sat herself down in an armchair by the fire. She seemed to have been swallowed by the chair; all that Annie could see were two thin legs and a pair of knitted slippers, but her voice went on, just as clear as it had been before.

'I would have given it to her, but she went and died and I didn't want him to have it. I do have to say I never took to whatshername. I wouldn't have wanted her to hide it away in a boxroom or some out of the way place. It's too good for that sort of treatment. You'll see.'

I'd better take the bull by the horns, Annie thought, get this over with, even if it means she will never show me my mother's picture.

'Erm, Miss Dundas . . .'

A door on the other side of the hall opened and Kevin came in carrying a tray. His aunt clapped her hands.

'Good man yourself. This is my nephew . . . but of course you've met him. He always produces coffee just at the right moment, like a conjuror. Hey presto, door opens, enter Kevin and coffee. I do hope you like coffee?'

'Yes, thank you. I—'

'Good, good, good. On the table there, Kevin, and would you pour it out like a good lad?'

'She'd talk the hind leg off a donkey,' said Kevin, putting the tray down. Annie smiled. 'I've brought a cup for myself. I thought I might be able to stem the flow.'

'Tut,' said his aunt.

'Because . . .' he picked up the coffee pot and waved it in her direction, 'there is a reason for Miss Ross, who said yesterday that I might call her Annie, being here. Ain't there, Annie?'

'Well . . .'

'And you have to come out with it quickly. No ifs and buts, no wells. Nothing of that nature. You take it black, if I remember correctly.' He passed her a cup of coffee.

'Thanks. I wanted to see your aunt. For old times'

sake. You were my mother's friend? When I heard that you were still . . . well . . . still alive, I thought I should just come and say hello. For—'

'Old times' sake.' He handed Miss Dundas a cup of coffee. She gave his wrist a slap. 'What was that for?'

'You know well. Don't tease poor Annie. Let her take her own time. Pay him no heed, Annie m'dear. I can put him out if you like.'

'Oh, no, that seems a bit extreme.'

'Whatever you say. I used to go over about twice a week. It was a good little half-hour's walk. I used to take the dogs. They're both gone now and I haven't replaced them. I'm too old to have young dogs, you see: they'd be heartbroken when I died, just as I was when they went. That wouldn't be fair, so I just console myself with my cats . . . and of course there's Kevin.' She laughed, almost the laugh of a young girl. 'Yes, about twice a week I would go over in the afternoon and then on other days she would hop into that daft car of hers and come over here. Always welcome. We used to swim in the summer in that pool he made in the stream. That was one of the good things he gave her. Sorry. Sorry. I didn't mean to . . .'

'That's all right. And you painted her?'

'Well, sketched really. While we talked I would sketch. She never seemed to mind and then after she was . . . not here any longer I painted . . . it's good, yes. I wish that she had seen it . . . rather *fin de siècle* and dreamy. It gave me great pleasure to paint. It still does just to stand and look at it. She was a lonely person, you know.'

'She was always going places, meeting people. She used to dash off in her car. I remember that.'

The old lady shook her head. 'No. No. No. She was always alone. She either came to me or else she would drive away out into the country. She would walk over Callary Bog, or climb up to the top of the Pine Forest, lonely places, and sing, or read a book or just stand and look at the view the world was offering her. County Wicklow is very beautiful, you know. Towards the end she would just go and sit in a pub and trail home after an hour or two and tell you all lies.'

'But why?'

The old lady shook her head. 'I don't know, m'dear. I never asked her questions. I thought she would tell me what she wanted to tell me, and that was all right by me. She never told me why.'

There was silence in the room while Annie thought about what Miss Dundas had said.

'I suppose I was too young.'

'I suppose you were.'

'I wish . . .'

'There's no point in wishing anything. What's done, m'dear, cannot be undone.'

'I don't quite know how to take this. I don't quite know how to put it. You think she killed herself?'

'Oh yes. I know she did that.'

'You mean she . . .'

'Told me? Yes. The evening before. She drove over here and we had a little drink and she told me then. She seemed happy to have made up her mind, happy to be leaving. The thought of peace and darkness gave her joy of some sort. It was getting dark when she left and I waved her all the way down the avenue and her hand waved back at me out of the open window. It was all hushed up, you know. Not a word got out. Your father never knew that she had been here.'

'But . . . you mean to say that you never tried to stop her? You never told anyone? You never . . .'

'I didn't do anything.'

'Isn't that illegal?'

'Oh, yes, maybe it is. But I happen to believe that our bodies are ours to do what we like with. Why drag on through this life in misery when there's an alternative? Hey? Why on earth do that?'

'A doctor might have cured her of whatever was wrong with her. Might have made her want to live.'

'Doctors.'

Annie was startled by the venom with which Miss Dundas spoke the word.

'I wonder . . . I wonder if she ever thought about . . . ever mentioned me?'

'My dear woman, of course she did. She loved you. She worried about you, but in the end she thought that you would be all right. If anyone can cope with that man, she said to me, Annie can. She's not like me, she has a will of iron. I can only run away, she can face the world. Remember.'

The word reverberated in Annie's head. It made her smile.

'He was a cold fish. Relations were broken off between us after she died. I didn't even show him the painting. I was afraid he might wangle it out of me. Of course he would have paid me, but I just didn't want him to have it. I don't care much for cold fishes. Anyway, I was wrong about him being a cold fish, because he already had Miriam up his sleeve. More to his taste than your mother.'

'Have some more coffee?'

She had forgotten that he was there and his voice made her jump. 'No thanks.'

'Aunt?'

'No thank you, dear.'

'Do you want me to go? Do you want to be more private?'

'No, no, no, no,' said his aunt. 'I didn't take to her at all, that Miriam one. I never called, you know, and she never called on me.'

Kevin looked bewildered for a moment and then settled himself into his chair. 'Aunt . . .'

'If you're going to stay you must not interrupt, unless of course you have something important to say. Relevant, I should have said, that's the right word.'

'Fair enough. I will be a silent witness.' He crossed his right leg over his left and closed his eyes. 'I will tell you, though, because I think it's relevant, what I think of Miriam. I only call her that here in this privacy; over there, beyond, she was Mrs Ross to me. Mrs Ross to us all. I couldn't stand her, but she was, still is, a gorgeous lady. He had taste, your dada, although if you'll excuse me saying so I didn't like him much either. Her eyes gave me the come-on, the first time we met, but something else warned me not to heed the eyes. I only wanted a job, a part-time job at that. I did not need what she seemed to be offering – that seemed like trouble.'

'You never said a word,' said his aunt.

'No. Where was the point? You would, very sensibly, have advised me against taking the job. I might have lost my rag and told you to mind your own business and I might have marched away, out of your life, and, Aunt dear, you do need looking after.'

'Pish and tush,' said the old lady, but she looked pleased.

'We seem to have drifted from my mother. I don't want to talk about or hear about Miriam. I suppose she made him happy, so I should be pleased about that. I barely knew her. Tell me why you hold doctors in such low esteem?'

'I don't think it's low esteem, I just hardly ever use them. I don't seem to have the need. If I catch a cold, Kevin brings me hot drinks in bed. What more do I need? I'll die some day soon; no doctor can stop that happening. I hate medical pills and potions, always have. My mother used to boil up herbs from the garden. A sort of a witch doctor she was – people used to come to her with their ailments from all round the place. A good witch, I would say, not the sort you meet in fairy stories.'

'She might have saved Mummy.'

'I don't think so. I don't think that anyone could have done that. Not even Sir Galahad on his white horse. She was too frightened by life.'

'You really do have to tell me why. I think I should know. Is that not a good enough reason?'

'Well, Aunt, fire away. I must say that curiosity is killing this cat too.' He opened his eyes and smiled at Annie. To her surprise she found herself smiling back.

Miss Dundas plaited her fingers together and stared at them for a while in silence.

'I don't really know where to begin,' she said eventually. 'So I suppose I'd just better tell you what she told me. Only little snippets here and there, and maybe I have put it together wrong. She had no mother; her mother had died when she was born. That was her first tragedy, the next being the nature of her father, who was really born out of his time. He was an explorer by nature and spent most of his life looking for empty patches of the earth where no human had walked before. He hardly gave his child a second glance; he even forgot that she needed him to give her a name before he was off on some journey to Outer Mongolia or somewhere inhospitable like that. She told me that he hardly ever came back, and once when he arrived in Dublin and called round to see her – she would have been about six or seven – he said, "And what name did they call you after all, child?" and when she said Jude he laughed and said, "I didn't know that any of my relations had a sense of humour." I was puzzled by his laughter, she said to me, and she was even more puzzled when he told her that St Jude was the patron saint of lost causes. End of that little story. So you see, my dears, she was born a lost cause and she died one. I hope the next life made her happier than the first one did.'

'Dada called her Juliet.'

'I suppose he preferred that,' said Kevin. 'Under the circumstances I think I would have too. Why don't we go for a walk round the garden?' He put his coffee cup on the table and prepared to jump up from his chair.

'No, please, no. I'd much rather stay here. Don't you think we're better off just staying here, Miss Dundas? I don't want fresh air or flowers or anything like that, I just want you to tell me what you know.'

'Quite,' said Miss Dundas. 'Kevin finds it hard to sit still for more than about ten minutes, then he has to be fidgeting around. If, dear man, you wish to go and fidget in the garden, by all means off you go.'

'I'll stay. I like listening to the stories you tell. I will control my fidgety limbs. I promise.'

His aunt laughed. 'Well, Jude – because she was known as Jude by everyone until your father came along and upgraded her – lived from pillar to post, with aunts and cousins, with a grandmother for a while . . . the only fixed star in her horizon was Nanny. The pair of them were shifted round Dublin. I mean to say everyone was kind, but no one was hers. She really never knew what bed she was going to be sleeping in from one week to the next. And then he sent her to boarding school; she must have been about eight, I suppose. Yes. About eight. And in the holidays she and Nanny went to whoever could take them. Is it any wonder she was a lost soul?'

Annie didn't know what to say. She just sat and stared at the fire for what seemed like ages and the two of them waited politely for her to speak.

'I suppose she was lucky to have Nanny, her fixed star, as you called her. Oh dear, I do feel I have been most neglectful towards her. I presume that Dada left her some money in his will. Would you know?'

'She's dead, m'dear. Died several years ago. Your father never liked her, so he packed her off with an annuity to live with her sister in Roscommon. I don't imagine she got much joy out of that.'

'There's worse places than Roscommon,' said Kevin. 'Think of the Yemen, Soweto—'

'Kevin!' His aunt sounded exasperated.

'Sorry.' He got to his feet. 'I think I'll go. There are things I should be doing. Round the place. Bits and pieces. Goodbye, ladies. *Orrevor.*' He bowed to each of them and galloped out of the hall. His aunt looked fondly after him.

'Such a dear boy. I'd be in an old people's home if it weren't for him. Or somewhere like that. He saved my bacon when he came along. All my other pretty distant relations were whispering and plotting, all in my best interests, you understand, and he just entered the scene and embedded himself in my yard, and he's been there ever since. I have a lady who sort of cleans and we all manage very well. It's wonderful. I shall die in my own bed and I will leave the house to Kevin. Do you think he's gay?'

The thought had not occurred to her. 'I hadn't really thought about it.'

'Not, of course, that it matters, well, not to me anyway. I just wonder from time to time why some nice girl hasn't snapped him up.'

'Maybe he doesn't want to be snapped up. Like you. No one snapped you up. He may be a loner.'

Miss Dundas looked sad and Annie thought that she had said the wrong thing.

'Go on with your story about my mother. If you don't mind.'

'I don't mind, m'dear. Not in the slightest. I didn't meet her until she was married to him and had come to live here. I went to call shortly after she arrived. She was a beautiful child – well, that was what she seemed like to me. A beautiful child dressed in grown-up clothes, and he – he came in just before I left – was as proud as Punch of her. He ate her up with his eyes; he wanted to be touching her all the time. Sweet-heart, he called her. And she would smile her charming smile at him and he would stretch out his hand and touch her arm.' She stretched out her hand and touched Annie's arm, her fingers lingering there for a moment. 'Like that.'

'Did she love him?'

'Oh, I think so. Yes, indeed she did. He was like a wonderful father figure. Someone she had always wanted in her life, returned to her by the gods.'

For a long time the two of them sat, not speaking, and the logs in the fire crackled and from up the hill at the back of the house a dog could be heard yelping, a high-pitched excited sound.

'Oh, dear,' said Miss Dundas. 'Someone's found something. I do hope it's not fox cubs. I hate to think of those sweet little animals being tormented by dogs. He was very handsome, you must remember that.'

'Yes.'

'Ladies liked him. I do have to say that he liked ladies too. Quite a name he had for that sort of thing. He held off for a while after he married your mother, but then . . .' She sighed. 'You know the way men can be?'

'And Mummy, did she find out?'

'She surely did, just when she was about to have you, to become the happiest person in the entire world. She was told by some blethering, scheming woman who should have kept her mouth shut. A woman who had had a little whirl with him in the past. You know the way women can be? Your poor mother's life fell apart again. The confidence she had built up just crumbled away.'

'Did she tell him?'

The old lady shook her head. 'I was the only soul

she told, and of course Nanny. Nanny knew her whole story. From start to end. No, no, no, she never breathed a word to him, she just closed up like a clam. She refused to go places with him, the clothes he gave her just hung in the press unworn, she never took the jewellery from the boxes. She paid him as little heed as possible and then little by little she took to the bottle. That was her companion, her dear friend.'

'She told you all this?'

'In fits and starts. And I observed. I thought at times I should talk to him about it, but then I thought, no, she wouldn't want me to do that. It would have been a breach of trust. I wanted her to trust me.'

'Even if death was her aim?'

'I'm afraid so, yes.'

Annie got up. She couldn't remain sitting there any longer. 'I think I'll go now. I have to think.'

'Will you come back?'

'I don't know.'

'I hope you do.'

'You helped her kill herself. She might be alive still.

She might have seen me grow up; that might have cured her. If she had waited. I would have had a mother, she would have had me. Our lives would have been so different. I could have minded her. Kept her safe. No, I don't think I'll come back. Thank you for the coffee.' She marched across the hall and opened the door.

'Don't you want to see the picture I did of your mother?'

'Yes. I suppose I do.' She shut the door again, then changed her mind. 'No. I don't think so. I'll go.' She opened the door again and went out into the rain. She got into the car and slammed the door and sat with her hands gripping the steering wheel. She shut her eyes.

Why the hell did that bloody old woman tell me that spiel?

Because you asked her to.

I did not. I was looking for comfort. No one asked her to. She just sort of wandered into it. She enjoyed telling me.

She did not.

Yes, she did. You could hear her voice lightening as her secret poured out.

Such rubbish you talk. Who are you anyway?

I'm you, you fool.

I suppose you must be. Yes.

There was a tap on the window. She opened her eyes. Kevin was standing by the passenger door. She pressed the knob and the window slid down. He stuck his head in. 'Are you OK?'

'Yes.'

'I just wondered.' He opened the door. 'Are you going over to the house? Your house?'

'No.'

'Where are you going?'

She switched on the engine. 'It's not your business where I'm going.'

'True enough. I just thought that if you would drive me to Dun Laoghaire I would buy you lunch.'

'No.'

'Well, drive me to Dun Laoghaire and I won't buy you lunch.'

'You have a perfectly good car of your own. And what about your aunt? You can't just whizz off and leave her alone.'

'My aunt and I do not live in each other's pockets.'

'I think she's upset at the moment.'

'You've upset her?'

'She upset us both. So if you don't mind . . .' She revved the engine. He hopped into the car and slammed the door.

'Now look here . . .' She turned off the engine. 'Haven't I made myself clear? I'm driving you nowhere. So please . . .' She waved her hand towards the door; he just sat there smiling.

'What have you got against me?'

'I have got nothing against you. I just want to be alone. I have to digest what your aunt has told me.'

He continued to smile.

'So . . . do you mind getting out?'

He shook his head. 'I'll just stay here. I'll just sit in silence, I promise you. If you don't want me to talk I won't open my mouth. I'll sit and look at passing traffic, fields, houses, people walking, women pushing prams. I'll store them in my head for a rainy day. I don't need to talk, but I do need to be with you.'

Annie was surprised. 'Well I don't need you to be with me.'

'You've had a shock. You must have someone near at hand. In fact I should probably drive. Yes. I'll drive.'

'You bloody well won't.'

'We'll just sit here so. Friendly like.' He smiled at her again; a bit like a wolf, she thought, or maybe a tyger, tyger, burning bright. 'Just until you've recovered your equilibrium.'

She reached out and turned the key and the car gave a little jump into life. She was angry. She didn't know what to do; worse than that she didn't know what to say.

'I'm a nervous passenger,' he said. 'So please don't drive too fast.'

'Hunh,' was all she said to that.

They drove in silence down the twisty road towards

Dublin. The branches of the trees formed a canopy of green above them; the wheels crackled on the wet road. A man walking his dog raised a hand towards them as they drove past and Annie smiled. She liked that. In England they only waved at you if they wanted a lift, but here it was some sort of brotherhood. Hello fellow traveller!

'Theo Jenkins,' said the passenger. 'Next-door neighbour.'

Blow that, she thought, so much for silly sentimental thoughts.

'Nice man. Gay as a bee. Plays the cello in the Radio Éireann Symphony Orchestra.' He was silent for a moment or two. 'If I was a musician I'd want to be a soloist. Wouldn't you? I've never wanted to be part of a crowd, even if they're making sublime music. In fact the more sublime the more I would want to be a soloist. Of course, I don't consider chamber music to come into the crowd category . . .'

'I thought you said you wouldn't speak.'

He shut up. He shuttered his eyes and slipped down

in his seat; he didn't look cross, just, perhaps, asleep. Anyway, they drove in silence for another ten minutes. *Sing a song of sixpence* jingled into her head, *a pocket full of rye.* Nothing more serious. *Four and twenty blackbirds baked in a pie . . .* now there were traffic lights and a bus. Houses lined the road, women pushed babies in buggies.

'I'm sorry,' she said. He remained ostensibly asleep.

The king was in his counting house, counting out his . . . the king was in the cemetery, weighted down by marble. Expensive marble chosen by Mrs number two wife, polished and gleaming, as he had been in life, always surrounded by polished and gleaming objects and people.

The queen . . . no, she was dead; no more eating bread and honey for her. She wished, she did wish that Miss Dundas hadn't told her that stuff. She wished that she'd kept her secret to herself. Of course it wasn't her secret, they all knew, except her. Nanny, Dada, Mrs number two wife, Mr and Mrs Cooke, the doctors, the clergy, everyone. Sorry for your trouble, they would have whispered to him as they shook his hand. Not a word to the child, this is not fit news for a child to be told. That would have been his order of the day.

She hadn't been a child for such a long time.

Dear daughter, he might have written to her in a letter to London, all those years later, when he might have considered her to be an adult, *I should have told you before, but I didn't think when you were so young it would be a proper thing to burden you with . . . it is not a very nice thing to burden anyone with at any age . . . but now I think it is best for me to tell you, before someone else does, the truth about your mother's death. She was as you know an unhappy lady. I think I might say a very unhappy lady. I thought when we were first married that I could make her happy. Perhaps all people about to get married think this, I don't know. Anyway I was wrong. I suppose I must bear some blame for not having tried hard enough. After you had gone to school that day, after you had said goodbye to her and she had said whatever it was she said to you, I'm sure it was something loving, she crammed herself full of sleeping pills and drifted out of this life that she appeared to hate so much. I hope that she is happier now wherever she may be. Nanny found her lying quite peacefully among her pillows at about twelve o'clock. I am sorry to have to write this letter to you. I hope you will bear the pain with your usual staunchness. I do hope that you will come over here and see me soon.*

She wondered if it had ever occurred to him to write her such a letter. She didn't think so.

Then she wondered if that was how it had happened. Had Nanny found her lying peacefully? Had she really drifted or had there been torment?

Of course there must have been torment, for her to decide to do it at all.

She drew the car in to the side of the road and found herself crying.

Damn.

The odd job man opened his eyes. He smiled, not at Annie, just a general sort of smile, out of the front window of the car.

'The rain has stopped,' he said.

'Yes.'

'We have stopped.'

'Yes.'

'You're crying.'

'Yes.'

'I knew you should have let me drive. Have you got a handkerchief?'

'Did you know?' she asked.

'Know what?'

'About my mother.'

He thought for a while. 'I suppose I did. Not that anyone told me, but I used to listen when they were talking among themselves. Why do you ask?'

'I just wondered if I was the only person in the world who didn't know.'

'Probably. Have you got a handkerchief? Your face needs attention. You were only ten or something like that after all.'

There was a very long silence between them.

'They were protecting you. You were too young to

be told that sort of thing and then when you were old enough there didn't seem to be any point. It had become the past, stuff for forgetting.'

'Do you really think we should forget the past?'

'Why not? There's nothing we can do about it. If you allow it to, it can destroy your future. Throw it away.'

'You can't be right to say a thing like that. We are our past.'

'Pish and tush.'

Annie laughed.

'Why do you laugh?'

'Your aunt says that. It's a pretty dotty thing to say.'

'Well at least it stopped the tears.'

She rubbed at her face with the back of her hand. 'I hate crying. I feel such a fool when I cry. And I look so awful, all red and snotty, not like the heroines in books at all. They seem to cry with grace.'

'That's where I say pish and tush again. Come on, drive on. There's a wine bar in Glasthule – we'll have a glass of wine and a bun or something and we can talk about the whole thing then. That is if you want to. Or I could just get out of the car now and walk back home. It's up to you.'

'It's quite a long walk and all uphill.'

'I can manage.' He put his hand on the lever to open the door.

'It's OK,' she said. 'We'll go to Glasthule. Maybe Glasthule will hold my fate." He slid down in his seat and closed his eyes again. 'Maybe Glasthule will hold my fate.' She repeated the words very quietly to herself. She started the engine and they moved slowly back on to the road.

The rain had blown away and the sun sailed across the pale blue sky, heading for the west, trailing behind it wisps of cloud, tattered lace, faintly tinted with gold.

The wine bar was painted a somewhat lugubrious brown. A few hardy smokers sat at some tables scattered across the footpath puffing their lungs out. Annie felt sorry for them; she felt glad that she was going past them into the darkness, where no one could see her red eyes, her crumpled face. A glass of wine would help; then she thought of Jude and wondered if she had loved the glass of wine before she started loving the gin. His hand was on her shoulder guiding her towards the door. She had been right: it was dark and filled with tables covered with wine bottles round which you had to make your way; beyond these tables were more of different sizes and shapes where people sat in indifferent comfort but quite happily. His hand guided her towards a small table in a corner where no one could trip over them or listen to their conversation.

'It's not the Ritz, but they make very good pâté and coffee, whatever sort you feel inclined to drink. Red or white?'

'Ah . . . yes . . . well, red please. I presume you mean wine.'

He was busy miming two glasses of red wine at a dark-haired girl and didn't answer.

'I shouldn't, I suppose. I'm driving.'

'One glass won't do you any harm.'

'I suppose not.'

He sat down beside her and took her hand. In spite of the fact that he was an odd job man his hand was soft; it lay over hers on the table like an expensive glove. She wriggled her fingers out from under the weight of his.

'No,' she said.

He smiled slightly. He didn't say anything. He lifted a hand and beckoned the waitress, who crossed through the tables and chairs, the shopping bags and sticks, with her smiling face into their silence.

'Sir?'

'Two glasses of Côtes du Rhône, please, and when you bring them we'll tell you what we want to eat.'

'Right you be, sir,' and she wiggled off through the furniture.

He turned towards Annie. 'Well . . .'

'My mother . . . ?'

'Yes.' He drummed his fingers on the table.

'You said . . .'

'Yes. I know what I said. I didn't mean it. I have

nothing to say. No bloody thing.' His fingers played an arpeggio on the table top. 'I just wanted to get in here and have a glass of wine. I wanted to get away from the aunt. I wanted to make sure that you were OK. I wanted—'

'Oh, do shut up.'

He looked a little hurt. 'Do you dislike me quite a lot?'

She felt her face getting red. 'I just didn't want you to hold my hand. People have their own views about that sort of thing.'

'It can be a comforting thing.'

'That depends.'

He nodded.

The girl appeared beside them with two glasses of wine. 'So?'

'I'll have a cappuccino and brown bread and pâté, please. How about you, Annie?'

'That's fine, lovely. I'll have the same.'

The girl nodded and disappeared.

'I remember when this place was just a bend in the

road, a couple of dingy shops and a cinema. It's posh now. Ain't it?'

'I don't remember it quite like that.'

'But you're much younger than I am.'

'I used to come and swim here. At the harbour. Most Saturday afternoons, and if it was raining we used to go to the pictures. How much younger? What age are you?'

He took a drink and rattled it round in his mouth for a while before swallowing it.

'Two years younger than she was,' he said at last.

'She?'

'I would have been sixteen when you were born. Sixteen. Still at bloody school.'

'Do you mean my mother? Is that who you mean when you say she?'

'Jude.' He took another drink from his glass and then put it down on the table with a little snap. 'Do you remember her?'

'Of course I remember her.' She was angry. 'Such a stupid question. Bloody stupid.'

He looked silently at her for a while, and the anger burned inside her throat.

'I'm sorry,' he murmured. 'I didn't mean to . . . Children make up their own faces for the people they love. I just wondered . . . well, if she came in the door this moment would you recognise her.'

The girl came back with their orders on a tray and offloaded them on to the table. Annie looked at her hands as she spread the cups and plates between them. The nails were bitten and painted with shiny polish.

'Did you see my aunt's painting of your mother?'

'No.'

The girl placed the last cup in front of Annie and stood looking down at them. 'Anything else?'

'No thanks.

She nodded and turned away.

'You should have,' he said.

'I should have what?'

'Gone and looked at that picture. It is your mother seen through my aunt's eyes. Maybe you wouldn't have recognised her. Look here.' He leaned towards her as he spoke. 'Let's gobble up this stuff and then we'll walk round to the harbour and I'll tell you what I know about Jude. That is if it's not raining, and of course if it's what you'd like to do.'

Annie nodded. Why not, she thought. That harbour has been a place of happiness for me, so why not?

He smiled and began at once to pile pâté on to the dark brown bread that the girl had brought.

'So, now we can talk about anything. About shoes and ships and sealing wax. Anything there you fancy talking about?'

She smiled and shook her head.

'Cabbages and kings?'

'We don't have to talk about anything. We can just eat in silence.'

So they ate in silence, well not quite silence; there was the soft murmuring of other people's conversations, little spurts of laughter, the tapping of metal on china and the clinking of glasses. Annie felt glum and probably looked glum. She felt as if she would never speak again, as though the words that normally rattled in her head had turned into enormous immovable blocks of black stone and from behind the stone she could faintly hear the voice of her mother singing.

'*Miss Otis regrets . . .*'

So far away. So very long ago. A song she had always hated. Annie used to cry and stick her fingers as far as they would go into her ears when Jude sang it.

'. . . *she's unable to lunch today.*' Then Jude would laugh. She would run her fingers in an arpeggio up and down the piano and laugh. 'So foolish you are, Annie darling. It's a brilliant song.'

Miss Otis . . . She pushed her plate away and stood up.

'Are you all right?'

'I'm sorry. I'm . . . Fresh air. I'll . . .' she moved away from the table, 'meet you at the harbour. Sorry. I . . .'

She ran out into the street where the sky was blue and the sun sparkled on the wet pavement and the voice in her head dissolved and the stones dissolved and normality slowly took over.

She sat in the car for a few minutes and then drove slowly round to the harbour.

A row of seagulls stood on the wall watching some children playing with a ball on the semicircle of sand below them. The birds didn't move. Their yellow eyes just stared as if made of stone.

God, I hate them, Annie thought. She got out of the car and slammed the door and walked towards the wall. Slowly they took off, one by one, and flapped their way to the other side of the harbour. She sat down on the wall and waited.

He came.

The first she knew of his arrival was when he sat down beside her on the wall; she hadn't heard his feet approaching.

'You must have Red Indian blood in you. You make no sound when you walk. You don't even seem to displace the air.'

'You'll get piles sitting on a wet stone wall.'

'That's an old wives' tale.'

'Some old wives speak truth. Do you mind if I smoke?'

'Not in the slightest.'

He took cigarettes from his pocket and a lighter. 'Do you?' He offered her the packet. She shook her head. Below them one of the children kicked the ball into the sea. It was a good hard kick and the large red ball started to float out towards the harbour entrance, with the falling tide.

'Oh, dear,' said Annie.

'What's the matter?'

She nodded towards the floating ball.

The three children were lined up at the edge of the water, staring out at the ball; then all hell was let loose. The smallest girl picked up a handful of water and threw it at the ball kicker, who laughed as the water sparkled harmlessly round him. Then she picked up some sand and threw it straight at his face. 'My ball,' she yelled as she threw. Kevin jumped down from the wall on to the sand.

'Hey, kids,' he shouted. He pulled off his trousers and his shoes and socks and walked sedately to the sea's edge. The children turned and stared at him. He handed his shirt to the smallest girl and walked into the water. 'I'll have it for you in a jiffy. It's much too beautiful a ball to let it go floating off God knows where.' He waved at Annie.

She waved back. 'Is it cold, Sir Galahad?' she shouted towards him.

'Fucking freezing.'

The children screamed with laughter.

Kevin walked towards the harbour wall. To begin with the water only barely reached his knees and then suddenly he was swimming and the ball was bobbing just in front of him. A young woman with a dog on a lead had joined the children and they all cheered when he got his hand on the ball, turned, and started swimming back towards them once more.

'He said a rude word.'

'We're going home, kids. We're late as it is.'

'A very rude word.'

He was walking towards them now, with the ball held triumphantly over his head. The dog barked.

'Just say thank you to the man and then we must go.'

'Very, very, very rude.'

He had reached them and with one hand he took his shirt from the little girl and with the other he presented her with the ball.

'Thank you,' she said, and then filled with shyness she turned and ran.

The girl with the dog handed him a towel, which had been hanging over her shoulder. 'It's a bit doggy,' she said, 'but better than nothing. And thank you, for being so gallant.'

He blotted at his arms and chest with the towel. 'No big deal,' he said.

'Well I'd have just let it go. I'd have bought her another.'

'Tut tut.' He handed her back the towel. 'Thanks.' He pulled his shirt on over his head.

The child who had taken her mother's hand and was swinging it backwards and forwards spoke again, very loud and clear.

'He did say a very rude word. A very, very, very. Didn't you?'

He smiled at her. 'I did indeed. I am famous for saying rude words. They pour out of me like water from a tap. Would you like me to say some more?'

She stopped swinging her mother's hand and stepped closer to her; she stared down at her sandy feet.

'I think we should go. Thank you once more. I hope you're not too cold.' The young woman turned and went back up the beach to where her other daughter stood holding her big red ball; the boy smiled at Kevin and followed them.

Kevin picked up his trousers and shoes and climbed up to where Annie was sitting. 'Life is full of surprises.'

'Are you frozen? There's a rug in the car. Don't put on your trousers until you're warm and dry. Go on, get in. Give me a shout when you're decent.'

When she got into the car he was fully dressed and had the rug draped over his shoulders. He was combing his hair with his fingers.

'That was a chilly little operation.'

'It was very nice of you to do it.'

'I'm an odd job man. It was an odd job.'

She laughed.

'Can I talk to you now?'

'If you're not too cold.'

He shook his head, shut his eyes and looked as if he were about to fall asleep.

'My parents,' he said after quite a long silence, 'were always of the opinion that my Aunt Katie, Miss Dundas to you, would leave me her house when she died, so every opportunity that offered, like half term or some such, they would pack me off to stay with her. "Fetch and carry for her," my mother would say. "Make yourself useful. Mend things, bring in the wood. You know. All the things you don't do at home." I have to say I never did anything at home. I had three sisters who I had well trained to fetch and carry for me. Anyway, I was staying with Aunt for a couple of days when I met Jude for the first time. I had been taking the dogs for a walk. We used to go out the back and through the woods and then up the road towards the Pine Forest. They loved that walk best of all. Am I perhaps boring you?'

'No. Not at all. I love being told stories.'

'My aunt says I digress, never stick to the point.'

'I am confident that you'll come back to the point sometime or other. We're not in any rush.'

'Well, there was this old crappy car sitting outside the front door and a baby crying in it. There on the back seat in a basket, just sort of murmur crying, not real yelling. I didn't know a thing about babies, so I went into the house to look for someone who did, and there was Aunt, sitting in front of the fire in the hall talking nineteen to the dozen to your mother.'

'So what did you do?'

'I just said, "There's a baby . . ." and this girl leaped up from her chair. "Oh, my God!" And she was out of the house like greased lightning. "What's the matter with her?" I asked Aunt. She just sat there looking surprised. "Should I . . ." "Do nothing. Absolutely nothing." Then we heard the baby crying and the soothing voice of Jude. "There, there, there." She sang the word. "There, there, there." And she came slowly into the room, holding the baby up against her shoulder.

"Miss Dundas, allow me to introduce you to Annie Ross." Aunt got up and held out her arms for the baby. With great care Jude placed the baby in her arms and the two women gazed silently at the child, who stopped crying and gazed back. "What a beautiful baby," said Aunt. Jude laughed. "Isn't she? And to think that I forgot about her. If it hadn't been for . . ." She turned and gave me such a wonderful smile that my heart almost stopped. I was only sixteen and no woman had ever smiled like that at me before. "My nephew, Kevin. Kevin, this is Mrs Ross, and Annie of course. You've met Annie."'

'"Jude, you must call me Jude. Please will you call me Jude?"

'What an ass I was. I just stood there and she shook my hand and kissed my cheek and I just stood there like a fucking eejit. Then it became unbearable and I pulled my hand away from hers and bolted out of the room. I slammed the door behind me and ran across the avenue and the lawn, with the dogs lolloping along behind me. I could hear the women's laughter echoing in my ears. I skulked around until I heard her car go and Aunt's voice calling for me. "You can come in now."

'She was standing by the fireplace. "What sort of game were you playing?" She sat down and picked up her book. "There's no need for you to answer. I had forgotten that you are still a child."

'I wanted to yell at her, to tell her that the most extraordinary thing had happened to me, something that I felt sure had never happened to anyone before, but I just stood there and stared at her and she attended to her book and then I left the room and went and lay on my bed and wished and wished that the whole afternoon could happen again and I could be grown up and strong. How am I doing? That's the end of act one.'

After a moment, Annie clapped. 'How long is the interval?'

'Do you want me to go on?'

'Of course. You said you were going to tell me about my mother, so far you've told me a tale about yourself. Maybe you've lured me here under false pretences.

Maybe you never met her again. If you have more to tell me, then tell me.'

It had started to rain again, tiny pearls that stuck on the windows, quivering, rather than running down the glass.

'I kept out of her way. For a couple of years I had to finish with school and then I went to college. I do have to say that I didn't enjoy college. I didn't get anything from being lectured to, I loathed doing exams, and none of the girls were as beautiful as my memory of Jude. So I went to England . . .'

How stupid we've all been, thought Annie, all running away, as if that solved anything.

'. . . and became an odd job man. I could have stayed there for ever, made quite a good business out of it, employed people. I could have become the chief executive officer of my own odd job company, but Dublin had its claws in me so after about five years I came back and here I am, and will be for ever. Except of course for the odd holiday. I love the beautiful cities of Europe. I love to go and wander in them, I love to see the animation on the faces of people talking in a language that I don't understand. My imagination—'

'My mother,' she interrupted.

'Yes.' He sighed and stared out of the window, through the pearls of rain. 'Bloody weather. This doesn't happen in other countries.'

'In other countries they have tornadoes, earthquakes, tsunamis, hurricanes. We just have rain. Be thankful.'

He laughed. 'Your mother. Jude. I went to visit Aunt about a week after I got home from England. They had been talking about her, my mother and father. They were worried about her living alone out there. Sleeping, you know, all night, out there, in the dark, with strangers wandering round. Daft talk really. Alone and old. They went on and on about it. So I went out on my bike to see if I could perhaps fix up an outhouse, somewhere that I wouldn't be in her way, but I would be there, if you know what I mean. It was summer. Yes. Real summer. Someone had just cut the grass and I could smell it as I pedalled up the drive. The hall door was open and I stepped in. It was dark and for a few moments I couldn't see, but I could hear a murmur of voices coming from the door that led out on to the veranda.'

He stopped talking and laughed a little uneasily, as if he were embarrassed by his recollection.

'I wasn't expecting her. I thought I had forgotten about her, recovered my equilibrium, grown up, some people might say, and there she sat in a wicker chair shading her eyes from the sun's light with her hand, her hair tied back from her face with a red scarf, and on her knee this huge straw hat. Aunt was standing at her easel sketching. A scene . . . a scene . . . to be remembered. She saw me, she looked straight into my eyes and blushed. Her neck, her face totally changed colour and I stared at her. I wanted to eat her, devour her, have her become part of me. I never thought I would hear myself talking like this. I never . . .'

'It's OK.'

He nodded.

'Do go on. What did Miss Dundas say?'

'I didn't hear her to begin with. She put down her

crayon and came over and kissed me. "Dear Kevin," she said, "how lovely to see you. They told me you were coming home. You remember Jude, of course." She gave me a slight push and I moved towards Jude. She held her hand out and I took it and bent and kissed it. "Well well," said Aunt, "London has improved your manners, no question." Jude held on to my fingers, ever so lightly. Her fingers were trembling.

'"How nice to see you again." She smiled at me and let go of my hand.

'"Erm, how's the baby?"

'She threw back her head and roared with laughter. "She's great. She's not a baby any longer. She's a small demon who rushes round the place at great speed. She wouldn't let you forget her now, if you wanted to. Annie. Her name is Annie. She goes to nursery school. She can write her name, and she knows how to skip. So!"

'"So indeed."

'"She's almost as clever as you are," muttered Aunt at me.

'Then we all went out into the yard and looked at

stables and a gardener's cottage and outhouses for me to live in and Jude chose the old tack room, which had a neat little fireplace downstairs and then stairs up to the floor above which we all thought would make a lovely bedroom. And that was that.'

He looked sad; he leaned forward and ran a finger down the windscreen. It made a squeaking sound and Annie's stomach turned over.

'Don't.'

'Sorry.' He took his finger off the glass. 'Sorry.' He stared remorsefully at the finger. 'Sorry.' He put his hand in his pocket.

'So then what?'

'She went home. I think she went home. She disappeared anyway and Aunt and I discussed whether I should come and live in her yard or not and we both thought it would be a good idea and she thought I should get to work right away on the tack room. "Why waste time?" then "What do you think of her?" all in one breath. "She seems nice enough." I tried to make my voice sound casual. Casual. You know, just as if it was any old girl she was talking about. "Do you want to come and look at the picture I'm doing of her?" "Yeah, sure. I'd like that." So I went over to the easel and there she sat with her hand shading her face from the sun, the straw hat on her knee, just as she had been when I went out on to the veranda, expecting something to happen, and I wondered if it was me she had been expecting, the expression on her face half delight, half fear, but also so beautiful.

'"What do you think? I mean it's not finished yet, but . . . ?"

'"Yes. It's very good." I could hardly speak; my voice seemed clogged. I felt a fool.

'She threw a cloth over the easel and said, "Come on, come on, let's go back and look at the tack room again."'

'So that's where you live? In the tack room? To this day?'

He nodded.

'Why didn't you move into your aunt's house? She's got lots of empty rooms.'

'I needed my own space. I don't like the feeling that I can be walked in on. Everyone needs a front door.'

'I'm sure she wouldn't have walked in on you.'

'She'd have had the right to. Anyway, for what it's worth, that's where I am. *J'y sùis, j'y reste.*'

Annie laughed. 'What a strange bloke you are.'

'Just an odd job man.'

'Don't you have any ambition? Don't you want to be someone, shine at something . . . I at least want to have a bookshop.'

'That's not very shiny.'

'It's something, some kind of dream.'

'Bookshops are closing by the minute. The world is changing. Soon there won't be any books, let alone bookshops. What will you do then?'

'I'll sit in my back yard and read all the books I will have collected. I'll become an expert.'

'In dusty tomes?'

'Probably.'

'Your father will turn in his grave.'

She felt a little stab of sorrow for Dada, or perhaps

it was just sorrow for herself, that she had no one left. 'He said he loved me.'

'Yes, yes, I'm sure he did. I shouldn't have said that. I never met him. Once or twice I saw him in the distance, that was all.'

She turned the key in the engine.

'Where are we going?'

'I thought I would show you the shop I want to buy. I'd like to know what you think of it. Mind you, if you think it's awful, I don't want to know.'

'I'll keep mum.'

There was a space just outside the shop and she pulled in. 'Well?'

He opened the door and got out.

'Where are you going?'

'In, of course. You have to go in. Come on.' He walked across the pavement and stood by the window, staring into the shop. The same two girls who had been there before were still there, still not selling expensive children's clothes. Unwillingly she got out and followed him. He took her arm and pushed open the door of the shop. The girls continued to chat to each other as they walked in. He looked around.

'It's small.'

'I'm used to small.'

'Can I be of any assistance?' One of the girls approached them.

'Well . . .'

He interrupted her. 'We're just having a look. We're thinking of buying the premises.'

The girl looked startled. 'The agent . . .'

'We thought we'd have a quick look round before we bothered him. You know, just check if it suited our needs. I hope you don't mind. I do hope . . .' He smiled at her. She turned to her friend.

'Do we mind?'

Her friend shrugged. 'We're here to sell children's clothes, not houses. We can't let you go traipsing round the property, that's the agent's job.'

'We don't want to go traipsing round, but if we could ask you a few questions . . . just one or two.' He smiled again. Annie examined a pale blue silk dress with blue and white smocking; one hundred and forty euros. God! Why did besotted mothers, grannies, aunts, do this? Dada would have. Yes, indeed he would; she wondered about Miss Dundas. She would seem to have her head screwed on the right way. Surely she . . .

'Annie. Hey, Annie. Ask a question.'

'Oh, sorry. How much space do you have?'

'Space?' She looked goofy.

'Yes, space, room space, like what's through that door?' Annie pointed at a door at the back of the shop. She saw that the odd job man was smiling. Bugger him anyway. The girl looked alarmed and turned towards her friend.

'Bernie . . .'

Bernie walked to the shop door and opened it. 'The address and telephone number of the agents are on the notice. I suggest that you get in touch with them. They will answer your questions. Good morning.'

Cowed, they slithered past her, out once more into the street. She shut the door behind them with a severe click. Kevin began to laugh and then Annie did too and they stood on the pavement and laughed and the two girls stared at them out of the window.

Two mornings later Annie was lying in bed. It had been still dark when she had woken up and she had lain gazing out of the window watching the daily ritual of the sky unfolding the world to those who want to watch, and have the energy to. That particular morning it was like watching some huge golden animal rising from its bed, pushing away the dark covers, almost imperceptibly, until at last the sky was lustrous, the sun free from the darkness.

Such silly mawkish thoughts whirled in her head and then the telephone rang. She looked at her watch. Eight thirty. Holy God, who would be ringing her at such an hour?

'Are you coming out to see my aunt?' His voice sounded bright, not as if he were still in bed.

'You woke me up,' she lied.

'It's a lovely day. I've been up for hours. I've walked

the dogs and cut a lot of grass and I'm just about to eat my breakfast. Come and join me.'

'Don't be silly. Maybe I'll get out later in the day.'

'I'm downstairs. I have a nice table by the window and I need someone else to come and stare at the flowers with me. Anyway, I never finished telling you about your mother. Are you a tea or coffee person?'

'I'm still in bed.'

'Well get up. I'll order your breakfast and it will arrive at the same time as you do. Coffee, I presume?'

'Tea.'

'Right you be.' He put down the receiver.

He hadn't spoken much about her mother. It had been mostly about himself, and she wondered was there more to tell, or did he just like the sound of his own voice.

It took her about fifteen minutes to do all the things you do to yourself in the morning to make yourself presentable to the world at large. He was sitting as he had said at a table by the window and staring out at the well-groomed garden. When she spoke he jumped as if she had stuck a pin into his arm. That made her laugh and the sound of her own laughter made her forgive him for hauling her out of bed at such an unholy hour.

'You startled me.'

'Serve you right. You should know at your age that social calls before nine in the morning are seldom welcome.' Annie sat down.

'I wanted to catch you before you set out. I thought you might take it into your head to visit my aunt today, and, well, I wanted to . . . well, stop you. So I came early.'

'Why?'

Two waitresses clattered breakfast dishes on to the table, tea for Annie, coffee for him, toast, bacon and eggs and all the rest.

'Thank you, thank you so much.' He gave them his smile.

'I'm not really a breakfast eater. I don't think I can manage all this.'

He reached over and poured a brown jet of tea

into her cup. 'Leave what you don't want. Personally I always work on the system of you never know when you're going to get another meal so eat up the one you've got in front of you.'

'Tell me why you don't want me to visit your aunt.'

He looked at the plate in front of him, waiting for the waitresses to go. His lips were tightly pressed together as if he were trying to keep the words in his mouth from spilling out. She put some milk into her tea. The waitresses' hands flickered backwards and forwards across the table, then suddenly they were gone. He looked at her, stared straight into her eyes.

'She doesn't know. I have never told a single person.'

'Told them what?'

He poured himself some coffee . . . this is all very slow motion, she thought . . . then put some milk in it, and a spoonful of sugar which he slowly stirred.

'About Jude.'

'My mother.'

'Jude.' He raised his cup and took a long slow-motion drink from it.

'Would you for God's sake tell me what all this is about. You're making me angry.'

'I loved her.'

'I know you loved her, you told me that the other day.'

'And there's the thing I don't want Aunt to know, or anyone, if it comes to that. She loved me.'

'How do you know?'

'She told me.'

Annie laughed.

'Laugh away,' he said. 'I'm telling you the truth.'

'I'll be the judge of that.'

'You can't. You don't know. You can't possibly know. She told me on a summer morning. She had met me at about ten thirty and we had driven up the windy road to the Pine Forest. She hadn't spoken a word all the way, which wasn't like her at all. Usually she chatted and smiled and sang little episodes of song. She had a very sweet voice and her hair hung down round her shoulders and on sunny days the sun made it sparkle, but this day she didn't talk and just stared out of the window. I tried talking to her and she would nod her head, but I didn't think she was listening so I shut up. I shut up. Yes, I shut up.' He shut up again and took another drink of coffee.

'Then?'

'Well, we arrived at the place where I usually parked the car and no sooner had I stopped than she was out of the car and away up, running through the trees, her feet strewing the pine needles to left and right as she ran. There was no sound, no people, no wind, no birds even, just that sigh you get from time to time in a forest. So I followed her up into the silence. It was warm and the smell of the needles was really strong. I was just beginning to think that I would never catch her, never see her again, when there she was sitting in a little clearing in the trees where some bright green grass had pushed its way through the needles. "I'm here," she said, "there's no need for you to run any more." I was puffing and panting like a pig and I threw myself down beside her and took her hand. "How fast you run," I said to her, "like a gazelle," and then I laughed because I thought of Yeats' poem. She muttered some words that I didn't get and I leaned my head down nearer. "I love you. Oh, Kevin, I do, I love you so much." And so that was that.'

He began to eat his breakfast and Annie thought about the pair of them in the Pine Forest, lying twirled together with the sun glittering through the branches, and then she realised it was no fairy story he was telling her. *My mother . . . Jude . . .* He suddenly spoke again.

'Do you realise that your mother was younger than you are now when she died?'

His words startled her. It was something she had never thought of before. 'Was she?'

He nodded. 'She was twenty-eight. We had been lovers for four years.'

'Lovers?'

He nodded again.

Annie felt sick. She didn't want her mother to have been anybody's lover. She didn't mind the whole world loving Jude, but she wanted to have been the only person that Jude really loved. Childish? Yes, of course. Pretty bloody childish.

'We were so happy.'

Annie tried to think back, to see her face, to recognise happiness in her smile, a spark of pure joy in her eyes. Too many years got in the way, too many muted recollections. She had been too young to notice other people's happiness. She could hear her light steps, feel the breath of her clothes as she moved past, remember the feel of her hand on her head and always the mysterious smell that was wrapped around her wherever she went. No more than that.

He was talking.

'I'm sorry,' she said. 'I didn't hear you.'

'Sometimes you look very like your mother. You seem to lose all sense of where you are. She used to do that too, she would focus inside her head. She was singing, she used to tell me. She used to make up songs in her head and sing them to herself.'

'I never knew.'

'I suppose you were a bit young to know.'

'Did she tell you lies?'

'No. What on earth makes you think she did?'

'She told Dada lies. She must have.'

His face reddened. 'I suppose.'

'Suppose my eye. You must have known. What did you think she said to him if not lies?'

He shook his head.

'Did you make up the lies between you that she told him?'

'Of course not. I don't know what she said to him. I never asked her.'

'Well I know. I heard what she said to him once and I believed her. And he was beastly to her and I hated him and she was drunk, looking back on it, and wearing posh clothes. Yes, he was beastly to her, but he believed her. She said she'd been having lunch with two girlfriends and they'd all had a bit too much to drink and had enjoyed themselves. I think he believed her. I was on the stairs. She didn't know I was there to begin with, only when she ran past me. Well, she wasn't running really, she was like limping quickly and she pushed me out of the way. "Go," she said, just like that. "Go." And then she started to cry. That wasn't all that long before she died. Two, three weeks. I don't remember. She hardly came out of her room after that.'

He had stopped eating; his hands lay flat on the table, one on each side of his plate.

'And you said you were happy.'

'Yes.'

'How could you have been happy?' She picked up her plate and shoved it over on to the next table. The thought of eating made her feel ill. 'Tell me.'

'We were happy, both of us, when we were together, and that was a lot of the time. He worked hard, and a lot of his work was social, which Jude hated, so when he was off working, playing, call it what you will, she was with me.'

She I looked at him with disbelief. 'And nobody knew? I don't believe you.'

'I'm telling you the truth. We took great care. We never went into town. We explored the hills and valleys of County Wicklow. We hid amongst the granite blocks below the railway line past Greystones, and we swam. That used to worry her because she thought he would smell the sea off her, and she would insist on being home in time to bath and wash her hair so there was no hint of salt left on her body, no evidence.'

'I suppose you taught her to drink?'

'You're angry with me.'

'Yes, of course I am.'

'There's no need, Annie, I tell you we were happy. I promise you that.'

'Happy people don't commit suicide, they don't become alcoholics, they don't cry, they don't say I am dying Egypt. How can you promise anything?'

'Are you going to eat your breakfast?'

'Don't be silly. How could I eat now?'

She started to get up, but he leaned forward and gripped her arm to push her back down into her chair.

'No. You're not going. You have to listen.'

'I don't want to. Lies. Lies.'

'I have told you no lies and I don't intend to tell you

any. Annie. You must believe me. You must listen to me.'

'What?'

'For over four years we were happy . . . well, as happy as was possible under the circumstances . . . and no I didn't teach her to drink; she loved wine and we always had a bottle on our picnics. It wasn't until much later that I realised that she was having the odd drop of gin at home. "To keep me amenable" was what she said to me when I asked her about it. I had noticed a tremor in her hand and I asked her why and she said, "It must be the gin." I laughed. I thought she was joking. Then she said "to keep me amenable" and I knew then, for the first time, that things were going wrong. I had been so absorbed in my own happiness, and I thought in hers, that . . . that . . .'

He turned away from her and stared out of the window at the neatness of the garden. The paths had been swept, the edges trimmed, and all the flowers looked as if they had been washed and polished.

'. . . that I never gave a thought to what her life might

have been like when she wasn't with me. Aunt and I used to go up to the house occasionally for tea, all formal, me behaving like a perfect visitor, and you would come in and we all sat in the drawing room and Jude would play the piano and sing songs for us, and we pretended, she and I, that we only met when Aunt was with us . . . and we made delightful, inconsequential conversation.'

'Lies,' she said.

'It didn't seem to us as if we were lying; we would laugh about it afterwards or whenever we next met. We did a lot of laughing.' His voice was reflective. 'I should have known better. I wasn't a besotted teenager any longer. I should have got the drift before I did. And then when I did say to her "You're not happy these days. What's up?" she just shook her head. She took my hand and then said "I love you so much" and we forgot about our conversation for a while. We—'

'Quite. You don't have to tell me everything.'

'I think I do, now that I've begun.'

'Are you not going to eat your breakfast?' It was the

waitress, looking at her plate with a face of disapproval.

'No thanks. No. I, ah, don't feel . . . I'm not really a breakfast eater. Thank you. I'm sorry if . . .'

'It's my fault. I ordered for her before she came down.' He smiled his nice smile at her. She picked up the plate and walked away. He looked at Annie for a long while without speaking.

'We go on?' he asked finally.

'Yes. Oh, yes, we must go on.'

He sighed. 'A few days after she had said that to me, about being amenable – or maybe it was a few weeks, not long anyway – she burst into a storm of tears. Where were we . . .'

'I don't care where you were.'

'. . . yes. On top of the bog, out along the Military Road it was. We had parked our cars by the side of the road. There was a little shed close by where we used to sit with our backs to the wall and eat our sandwiches in the sun, but this day it was raining. Bucketing. Everything was dripping and grey all round us and we were in my car, quite cosy, and then she began to cry. I hugged her really tight to me and waited and waited until she stopped. When she did stop she looked like a poor little battered thing.

'"I'm pregnant."

'Her voice was muffled and I didn't think I'd heard her properly. "What?"

'"Pregnant."

'I was filled with such joy that I felt I was going to explode. "Darling, darling. Oh, my darling." She began to cry again. "What are you crying for? Now you must leave him. You must. We will be together. We will go wherever you want in the world. Odd job men are always welcome. Don't cry. Please don't cry."

'She shook her head. "There's Annie. I can't go anywhere without Annie. He won't let me take Annie away. I know that, for sure. I can't go. You'll have to go. He'll find out if you don't go. I'm always just on the verge of confessing it all to him myself, just teetering on the verge."

'"But why?"

'"I don't know. It would be a disaster and yet the

words are there, just behind my lips, struggling to get out. I can't leave without Annie. Therefore I cannot leave, therefore . . ."

'"We'll go straight away. Today. We'll collect Annie and we'll go."

'"We can't do it. I've thought and thought. There is nowhere we can go. Annie doesn't have a passport, mine is in his office . . ."

'"England. We can go there. We can hide. He won't find us."

'"Of course he will and he will take her away and I will never see her again."

'"Listen, Jude, be sensible . . ."

'"No. You must be sensible. We can't go anywhere. I must . . . well, this baby inside me . . . I must . . . You must help me and then when that is over, done with, we must not see each other again. You do know what I am trying to say?"

'Of course I knew. And of course I couldn't let her do it. "I can't let you do this."

'"You have to." Her voice was strong. No sound of

tears. "I wouldn't know where to start. I'd have to ask help from someone and I don't want to do that. I can't do that. No one in this country can keep a secret. So if you love me you must help me. Please, Kevin, please."

'"Darling, of course I'll help you. But we need to talk more about it. There must be some other solution."

'"No. No talking. It must be done at once. You must organise it . . . and no back-street witches with knitting needles." She looked straight into my eyes. "You do know what I'm talking about, don't you?"

'"Yes."

'"And you will help me, won't you?"

'"Of course."

'"No prevaricating."

'"I will do exactly what you ask me to do."

'She leaned forward and kissed me. "Go now," she said. "There's no point in wasting time."

'"Go?"

'"Yes. Go. I want this all over, behind me, done with. Oh, please, Kevin, go."

'Her voice was trembling. I thought she was going to cry again.

'"Find someone. You will, won't you? You won't just abandon me?"

'I got out of the car and went round and opened the door for her. I held out my hand and she took it and got out of the car. She stood very close to me for a moment and then turned and crossed the road to where her own car was parked. She stood with her hand on the door looking at me.

'"I really love you," she said and opened the door and got in. I watched her drive off and wondered if I would ever see her again. Then I drove back home to try to find an abortionist.' He whispered the word as if he were trying to wipe it out of his head.

Annie thought it best to remain silent. They were the only people left in the dining room; someone had opened the windows and the curtains swayed gently in the wind. She felt cold. Nothing to do with the weather; it was his story that had frozen her.

'So,' he said at last. 'I found someone for her. A

decent man, so I was told. In those days it was hard to imagine that anyone who did that was decent. I made an appointment for her to go and see him. I phoned her, which was something I had never done before. She sounded weird, angry, as if she hated me. She said very little. I could hear the scratch of the pencil as she wrote down the address. Then I asked her if she wanted me to come with her. "No." She snapped the word at me as if I had suggested something totally evil. I just wanted to be with her, to make sure that she was safe. I was wondering how to explain this to her and suddenly she spoke again. "Darling, darling Kevin" was what she said, and she put the receiver down so quietly that I didn't hear the click. I just heard emptiness. I never saw her or heard her voice again. Occasionally, though, I still hear her whispering those three words.'

'That's the end?'

He nodded. 'Two weeks later Aunt telephoned me and told me she was dead.'

'Where were you?'

'Bristol.'

'Bristol?'

'Yes. I'd worked there before. I knew the feel of the place, its highways and byways so to speak. I probably would have stayed there for ever if it hadn't been for Aunt. I couldn't bear the thought of her living there alone. I knew that with the best will in the world they would have put her in a home. She's a great old girl. You mustn't be too angry with her. Not angry at all, in fact.'

'I'm not angry. I was shocked. Maybe it seemed like anger, but it really wasn't. I didn't mean to be rude. I'll go and see her.'

'Whatever you say to her, don't tell her about me. Please.'

'She doesn't know? You mean to say that you were carrying on under her nose and she never knew? That I don't believe.'

'I don't like the expression carrying on.'

Too bad, Annie thought, too bloody bad.

'Jude might have told Nanny, but I don't think she did. No one knew.' He gave a little laugh. 'Only the dogs. They used to come in the car with me and run, and eat our sandwiches. They never told a soul.'

'When Miss Dundas rang you, in Bristol, and told you that . . . umm . . . my mother was dead, what did you do?'

'I cried.'

She didn't say a word.

'I couldn't stop. I don't know where the tears came from. I didn't know that it was possible to manufacture so much water. And when I did stop, several weeks later, I threw my stuff in my bag and went to the airport. I have never been back. This is my lot now, I said to myself, minding Aunt and grieving. I still grieve, you know. Sometimes when I am least expecting it I get stifled by a great black cloud of sorrow. Black.'

He got up from the table and walked over to the window.

'Then later – much, much later – Aunt told me what she told you. Of course I didn't believe her. I couldn't believe her.' He banged angrily on the glass with his fingers. 'There's still a part of my head that doesn't believe her. I play back in my mind every word she told me of their conversation the night before she . . . she . . . Jude . . .' He turned and stared at her. 'I'm sorry,' he said. 'Really, really sorry. I should never have brought the subject up.' He thumped at his forehead with a clenched fist, muttering, 'Never, never.'

Annie laughed.

'What are you laughing about?'

'We've gone a bit melodramatic, haven't we?'

'Rot. I'm not feeling melodramatic. I've told you that story the best way I can. No histrionics. I've been calm. On the outside, as calm as I can be. Yes.'

Annie felt sorry for him, and Jude, and herself; she got up and went over to him and put her hand on his shoulder. 'It's all so far in the past.' No reaction. She removed her hand. 'I suppose I'm sorriest for her. She couldn't cope. She had no knowledge of how to cope. She knew that death would solve her problems. She didn't think about fighting. Perhaps Miss Dundas might have helped her, if she had told her the truth. What do you think?'

He turned away from the window, from the sun-splattered flowers and the sea beyond. 'I suppose she might. She'd have done a lot of yelling. She yells when she's annoyed. She can be quite scary. But she's good, I mean really Christian good, not . . . well, you know. She would have yelled at Jude and yelled at me and having done that she would have settled down to try to resolve the problem. She'd probably have gone to see your father.'

'That wouldn't have got her very far.'

'You never can tell with Aunt. She would have stopped her . . .' He turned back once more towards the garden. 'Stopped her.' He repeated the words. 'I didn't know you at all then. I only saw you those few days we went to tea with your mother. You were a quiet little girl. You handed round the cake very politely. You used to shut your eyes when your mother sang.'

'I don't remember that. I wonder why I did that.'

She shut her eyes and tried to think herself back into the drawing room, the afternoon sun gleaming on the

Steinway, on the silver teapot, on the flowers, great bowls of flowers. All that she could see with her mind's eye, but she couldn't hear Jude's voice singing. She couldn't see her white fingers dancing along the keys. She wondered what she had sung, not the songs anyway that she had sung for her, not 'Miss Otis Regrets', no, she wouldn't have sung that for them. Nor 'Sing a song of sixpence'.

'I thought I'd go up to the house today. I thought I should have a look through Dada's things, see what can go and what should be kept. Mind you, she's probably done it already but there might be things that I would want to keep.'

'I can give you a lift. I'd go away and leave you in peace and then I could drive you back here. We might have dinner . . .'

'That's very kind of you, but no thanks. I don't want to be a bother.'

'It wouldn't be a bother, but suit yourself.'

'You think I'm a rotten driver, don't you?'

He laughed. 'Whatever gave you that idea?'

'I'd have you know I'm a bloody good driver. Not a knock or a scratch, clean licence.'

'There's lots of time ahead.'

'Well, think what you like. I'm going now.'

'What about dinner?'

Annie thought about dinner. After all, she thought, why not? 'Yes. That would be nice.'

'Good. I'll pick you up here about quarter to eight.'

'Thank you. I'll have made up my mind by then.'

'About what?'

'Just things.'

She left him standing by the window and went up to her bedroom to collect coat and bag and comb her hair tidily, in case. In case of what, she wondered.

Just things.

Two silver cars sat neatly by the steps when she arrived at the house.

What was the man's Scottish name?

She walked slowly up the steps trying hard to call it to mind. As she approached the door it opened and the man whose name she could not remember bowed her into the hall.

'Miss Ross, good morning.' He must have read her expression. 'James Fraser.'

'Good morning, Mr Fraser. I've just come to collect some stuff of my father's. I hope . . .'

'Not at all. There are two clients just having a wander. I've shown them the place and now they must have a little poke around on their own. A whisper.'

'I have to look for something in my father's study. You won't mind, will you? I won't disturb their whispering.'

'No, no. No problem at all, Miss Ross. Don't rush yourself. Take all the time you need.'

Dada's study was upstairs, next to his bedroom. 'The king is in his counting house,' Jude used to whisper to her, 'and must not be disturbed.' She would tiptoe across the landing and down the stairs and now she found herself tiptoeing up the stairs and across the biscuit-coloured carpet with its scattered brightly coloured rugs, the same as it had been then; her mother had scattered colour in every room. Annie heard the murmur of the viewers' voices as she crossed the landing, coming from the room that had been hers. She raised her hand automatically to knock at Dada's door when she reached it, but remembered in time and turned the knob instead and went in, closing the door behind her. It was a charming room, but as the rooms downstairs had been it was stripped of most of its furniture. Between the two windows was a tall thin bookcase, filled it seemed with squat black books, each with gold figures on its spine By one of the windows was an armchair, angled for gazing, with two large silk cushions to keep your back comfortable. She wondered had he ever sat in that chair and wasted his time by staring out of the window and couldn't believe that he had, but then she knew so little about him. There was still a faint smell of cigar smoke and something nameless but medicinal hanging in the air.

She peered at the books; the gold numbers on the spines were dates going right back to 1950. Diaries?

Of course diaries.

Soft leather covers like ladies' gloves. She took one into her hands. Her fingers trembled as she opened it, saw his writing, the fine strokes in the black ink he had always used. She wondered what had happened to his fountain pen. It had been silver, with his name on it and a date; she couldn't remember the date, nor why it had to be commemorated by such a fine present.

Remember.

She could not, only that he had always carried it in the inner pocket of his suit. She could see now his fastidious fingers plucking it out and laying it neatly on the table beside him.

Remember.

No. She could not.

She turned a page and his name was written on the flyleaf and after it the date. 1978. Curlicued, neat. Four years before she was born.

Flick, flick.

Thin pages with fine blue lines.

10 May. I have just received a telephone call from the nursing home to tell me that my father is dead. I am writing these words in order to gather myself together before I announce his death to the office staff, and then to the world. He was a hard man but a fair one, and his last six months have been painful for him and us as we watched his suffering. May God give him peace. I do have to say that his plan for me was the right one, and for that I thank him, will always thank him. I have no tears. He will be glad to have left the world as he had come to know it . . .

Then a whirl of empty pages. His equilibrium must have deserted him for quite a while, she thought.

14 November. I have toured the world. I have seen to it that wherever I have an organisation the wheels are oiled, the staff is happy, the right men are in the right places. They all know my face and they know that I act and listen with attention. Like my father I am a fair man, but not so hard. Things will go well, my way. He will see that from wherever he may be. I laugh to myself as I write those words. I feel stronger now, which is good. The time has come to settle my domestic life; a house, a wife and a son, these are what my life needs now. What every mature and successful man needs. When all the arrows are pointed in the right direction . . .

She put the book back on the shelf. She wondered if she wanted to read her father's diaries; by and large she thought not, but then . . . She took two at random and carried them over to the chair. She sat down and placed the books on her knee.

The king was in his counting house . . . counting . . . counting . . . *counting out his* . . . 'Oh, shut up,' she said aloud, 'just shut up.'

She heard the people talking quietly to each other, she heard the creak of the stairs. She opened one of the diaries.

3 September, Miriam's flat in Monaco. Here we are, and the sun is shining, the yachts clinking and dancing below us in the harbour, all spit and polish. Holidays in the perpetual sun. She has gone to get her hair done, gilding the lily I said to her as she left, and she laughed. So I have time to write in my diary, to read the pink paper, to slop around in my slippers, to drink a cup of coffee. To stand on the balcony and breathe in the scented air and to wonder why I left this form of luxurious living so late. Too late? I mustn't think of that. I must enjoy to the best of my ability what is left and when I feel my heart scurrying inside me like fifty mice in a cage I must just sit quite still and order it to stop, to calm down. My orders are normally obeyed. I think of the girl from time to time and wonder if she would enjoy this place, enjoy for a week or two this divinely useless way of life. Should I invite her? What would Miriam's reaction be?

She shut the book. Would I have gone, she wondered, if he had invited me? I would probably have remained snotty. If he had told me that he was ill, that might have been a different kettle of fish. I wouldn't have gone to Monaco, but I would have gone to visit him at home. Here.

Here.

Home.

His home.

Below her the front door opened and she could hear them talking on the steps, a woman's laughter rising and then drifting down into almost a whisper. They moved down the steps and crunched across the gravel to their car, Mr Fraser crunching beside them. Annie's attention turned once more to her father's diary.

14 December. A Christmas card arrived from the girl. I will send her five hundred pounds, and I will not tell her what the doctor has said. I will, in fact, not tell anyone what the doctor has said, not even Miriam. How do you know if doctors tell the truth or not? Anyway, my life, my way of life, is my own affair. I will make sure that all is properly ordered. We will go to Monaco for Christmas and will I hope rejoice in sunshine for two weeks, much better than medicine, injections, routines and soothing words. Soothing words tend to infuriate me. Am I, I wonder, becoming an irascible old man? There is so little time left, it would be a pity to waste what there is on irascibility. When we come back I will write and invite the girl over here.

Two car doors slammed and then the car was driven off down the avenue. She heard Mr Fraser come back up the steps and close the hall door. She flipped through the last few pages of the diary; they were blank. She heard his feet on the stairs and then the door opened and he came into the room.

'Satisfied customers,' he said. 'They were really taken by the place. The price may be beyond them, though. You see, to date there's no permission for development. If there was permission you'd be sitting on a goldmine.'

'Well I hope no one ever gets planning permission. The place would be ruined. I hate that thought.'

'It would depend. Some developments are very good. Very tasteful.'

She laughed. He looked mildly affronted.

'Sorry,' she muttered. 'It doesn't apply here, anyway. By the way, I'm not very good with money, I'm a bit lazy about it, but how much are we asking for the house? Mr O'Brien deals with all that sort of thing and I never asked him. Perhaps you could tell me.'

'Yes, of course. Five.'

'Five?'

'Million. Of course.'

She laughed again. *Who wants to be a millionaire?* she sang in her head. *I do.* Well anyway, whether I do or don't, I'm going to be.

He was talking. '. . . we could probably get more. It's in most excellent condition. Walk-in condition, and the grounds . . . we might get more.'

'Five sounds OK to me.'

'Euros, of course.'

'Of course.'

'Did you find what you were looking for?'

'Yes. Thank you. I did. My father's diaries. They're not of any interest to anyone but me.'

'I suppose not. I'll be off so. You'll lock up, won't you?'

'Yes. Look, you wouldn't mind carrying some of these down and shoving them in the back of my car? That would be terribly kind. Then we could both leave at the same time and you wouldn't have to worry about me locking up.'

So together they brought the diaries out to her car, he locked the front door, and she drove off.

Who wants to be a millionaire? sang her head. Well, I do.

One of the black books fell from the seat on to the floor of the car as she bumped to a stop outside the hotel. She picked it up and opened it.

4 April. The birth day. The child is not as I expected. It is a girl. I suppose I will get used to this eventually, and all one can say is better luck next time. I haven't yet seen her with her eyes open. She just lay in the little cot and looked pink and Juliet said, Pick her up, why don't you?

And Josie, who I presume will live with us for ever now, picked up the little creature and held her out towards me. I let her put the child in the crook of my arm and stared at the pink infant face.

You will love her, won't you? Please love her.

Yes, of course I will.

She's going to be so pretty. Look, she's got eyelashes and such big eyes. Next time you come we will tell her to open her eyes. Open your eyes for Dada I will say and you will fall in love with her.

She laughed. She looked so beautiful; I didn't think I would ever love the child as I loved the mother. Josie took the baby and put her back in the cot, tucking, wrapping, stroking the little face and crooning some unnamable song as she did so.

When will you be home?

I suppose in about a week. They like to keep rich people in for a week anyway. The rest they send home in twenty-four hours.

Just suppose the very rich people want to go home . . .

I think we'll call her Annie. Annie's a good name. Wasn't your mother's name Ann?

Yes.

There you are. That's settled. I don't think she needs another name. Do you?

I suppose not. But isn't it normal . . . ?

What's normal for God's sake? We're not normal. Now, off you both go and leave me and Annie to get to know each other. I shall sing to her and have her in my bed with me. All sorts of things that Nanny will never allow when we go home. Kiss me, darling, a nice gentle, soft kiss. Come back very soon.

So I gave her a gentle, soft kiss and Josie and I went home.

Should I cry, Annie wondered. She closed the diary and put it into her pocket. On the back seat of the car was a large plastic shopping bag, and she shovelled a lot of the books into it. She couldn't make her mind up whether she wanted to read her father's diaries or not. Would it not muddy the waters more than they were already muddied? Muddy and muddle.

Perhaps, on the other hand, she might find some warmth in her father's words, something she could love.

Hmm.

She hauled herself and the bag out of the car and went into the hotel. Upstairs in her room she laid the books carefully on the bed in the correct order and sat down and stared at them.

She finally reached out and took one.

17 May. I said to her at dinner time that I would like her to come to Ascot with me. She smiled her beautiful smile at me and at the same time shook her head.

But why not, darling? You can buy some lovely clothes. You will be the belle of the ball. It's a very glamorous occasion.

There's Annie . . .

Don't be silly, my darling. Annie will be well minded. Josie will look after her like a princess.

No, I must be here for her. I couldn't bear to leave her. You must go, of course you must. No one was ever there for me, only uncles and aunts, no real person. And look at the mess they made of me. I couldn't bear to go away from her for even a week without being able to explain that I was coming back again. You can't explain that sort of thing to someone of one. You must go and have a wonderfully happy time. I will be happy here and Annie will too.

That was that. We didn't speak about it again. I will go to Ascot and I will have a wonderful time. This yearning after baby stuff doesn't appeal to me at all. Her place should be at my side. I must insist on this. When I need her in the foreground, she must be in the foreground. She was so fresh, so young and charming when we were first married that I let her get away with her childishness. I was enchanted for a while by her adoration of me, and her playfulness and the way she would, for no reason, burst into song, the joy with which she received any presents I gave her, like the Steinway with which I replaced the old upright that she brought here with her, and the swimming pool that I made for her by damming the stream. I thought her heart would burst with excitement when I took her down to see that, the day the men had finished it. She was so happy, she clapped her hands and sang.

What a wonderful man you are, so full of kindness. I love you so much. And you must love me. Do you love me?

And I assured her that I did.

More than anyone else?

And I assured her of that too.

Then she put her hand on my arm and said, Remember.

Remember what?

You must always remember good moments as well as bad ones. That's what keeps you going on. Sometimes I find that hard to do. I get swamped by memories of loneliness and fear and I get afraid that I will never again have a lovely moment to remember.

I will keep you safe.

I hope, I do hope, that you will.

I often wonder if it is that old Miss Dundas who puts such thoughts into her head. Maybe I should tell Juliet not to see so much of her.

* * *

That comment annoyed Annie and she shut the little book with a snap. Why was he always tempted to interfere in other people's lives? She opened the diary again.

I came back on the late plane last night. Cooke met me and drove me home; we arrived about quarter to twelve. The drawing room lights were on and I heard the sound of the piano the moment I opened the door. It was something by Schubert and I stood for a moment or two in the hall and listened. She played with great confidence. Why can she not live with that confidence? I crossed the hall and opened the door, and she was so absorbed in the music that she didn't hear me come into the room. She was in her dressing gown and its silk sleeves fell softly about her wrists. She looked up from her dreams or whatever it was that absorbed her so intently and saw me. She smiled and lifted her hands from the keys.

I'm so glad you're back, she said gently and for a moment I felt a tiny twinge of guilt.

Today I came home for lunch. This is not something that I

usually do; lunch is a good time for a certain sort of work, making new acquaintances, entertaining what they call visiting firemen, meeting politicians, sometimes even secrets not for driving home to your family. However, that's what I did. Josie and Mrs Cooke were eating in the kitchen, no sign of Juliet.

She's up in the nursery with the wee lassie, said Josie. She likes to have a little time on her own with her.

Has she had her lunch?

She's had some fruit, sir, and a cup of coffee. Her usual. Can I get you something?

Some coffee and cheese and biscuits would be fine. No rush. Finish your own first, Mrs Cooke. I'll have it in the drawing room. If one of you would tell her that I'm there.

I left them to their own devices and went to wait for Juliet. Time passed and the rain started to drizzle down outside. After quite a long time, after I had eaten my cheese and drunk my coffee and was, in fact, just about to ring for Cooke and make my way back to the office, I heard her steps on the stairs.

She opened the door and came into the room. She was wearing a long robe and carried a towel over her shoulder.

How strange, was what she said. Nanny told me you were here and I didn't believe her. Are you all right? Is something the matter with you?

I'm fine. I just thought I'd come home and see you. A little surprise.

Indeed. I was just going for a swim.

In the rain?

Why not? It isn't cold. Why don't you come too?

No. I must get back to the office. I just wanted a word with you. Won't you sit down?

No. I can hear as well standing as I can sitting. Is this something serious? Should I be very anxious? She smiled a bright little smile at me.

Just something I've been wanting to say for a while. About Miss Dundas.

Oh yes? What do you want to say about her?

It seems to me that you see too much of her. It's not right that someone of your age should be . . .

What's age got to do with it? She's my friend.

You should have friends of your own age. You should see people of your own age. She makes you mournful.

She does not. If I am mournful it is my own nature. She is a wonderful, kind, intelligent woman. I am lucky to have such a friend.

Her eyes filled with tears.

It is only for your own good that I am saying this. I would like to see you thriving and happy.

I am happy. I promise you. May I go and swim now?

What am I to do with her?

Leave her to stew in her own juice. That is what my father would have said. Meanwhile . . . meanwhile you must lead the life you wish, with, of course, all possible discretion.

Then empty page after empty page. Just the occasional note.

The child started school today. Will things change for the better?

Juliet has decided to have a room of her own. This I presume means that we will have no son. I must spend some time with the child we have; I see no reason why a girl should not become a leader in finance. It must be a question of training.

I offered to give Juliet a new car for her birthday. She thanked me profusely but said no. I love my old jalopy was how she put it.

She goes out more now than in the past. She has secret friends whom she meets for lunch or goes to the cinema with. They don't come to swim in our pool. I asked her why not and she just shrugged and said, Some people don't swim unless the water is truly warm. They are, I think, old school pals.

We had a conversation at dinner last night: Tell me about your friends.

My friends?

Yes, the ones you spend your days with.

Oh, yes. Oh yes, them. She shut her eyes for a few moments and then opened them wide and smiled at me.

They're not very interesting. You wouldn't like them. Definitely. You wouldn't. Like them.

Just their names then.

She held five fingers up in front of her face.

Well, there's Annabelle, Marie-Louise, Helen and Kate and

Shirl . . . that's really Shirley, but we call her Shirl. Any other information that you want?

Where do you go? What do you do?

We hang out.

I don't know what that means.

She poured herself a glass of wine.

Anything you want it to mean. We don't do anything in particular; sit around and chat, walk up and down. She paused for a long time. Sometimes I go to concerts, but I do that on my own. Yes. I do that on my own. Sometime, when she's older, I will bring Annie to concerts. You must learn the ways of music when you are young. She stood up and picked up her glass from the table. Now, if you don't mind, I shall go to bed. Good night. She bent down and kissed my forehead and I got the smell of drink from her and I felt angry.

Annie didn't want to read any more. She packed the diaries back into the plastic bag and pushed it into the wardrobe. Why, she wondered, did people keep diaries. In order to remember? She heard her mother's voice whispering round the room. Remember.

She never took me to a concert. I would have liked that. I would have sat like a grown up and listened. I would have learned the ways of music. I would have pleased her. Yes, I think I would have done that.

Annie stared out of the window, at the flowers nodding and swaying in the gentle wind. What should I do, she wondered. Go to Merrion Square and consult Mr O'Brien?

That would probably be the most sensible thing to do. He was, surely, a well-balanced and decent man, with no axe to grind as far as she was concerned.

Go back to London? If she was going to do that she must write Mr O'Brien a note and he would see that everything went all right. He would keep an eye on the agent. He would be well paid. Yes.

Pals are more important than the past.

Do I believe that or not? I don't know. I find this place so unsettling. Ghosts, whispers, old memories of unhappy people. I think I prefer the constant hum of London, the dirt on your hands at the end of each day, the different colours of people's faces, the geraniums on my window sills, the rumbling from the underground late at night, 'Mawnin lav' from the man who sweeps the street as I set off on my bike each morning. And of course pals.

She took her mobile phone from her pocket and tapped out a message on it. *Back soon. Keep my seat warm. A.* She sent it.

She took the bag out of the wardrobe again and looked into it. She rummaged for a moment and then pulled out one of the books which she put on the table beside her. She flicked the pages over with a finger, empty page after empty page and then, suddenly his black sloping writing was there for her to see.

This is all. This is the end. I will write no more.

Dr Keane called round to see me this afternoon.

On chance, he said.

He was lucky to find me in. I have little desire to be in this house at the moment. Work is supreme. When I am working I can clear my head of all this stuff, this damned stuff that has been torturing me since the post mortem. I have kept it locked tight inside my head.

Anyway he said on chance, and I offered him a drink, which he accepted. I had one too and we stood for a long time quite silently staring at each other.

'She never told me about the baby,' he said at last. 'It came as quite a shock to me. I hadn't seen her for months.' He walked over to the window and looked out over the city below us. 'Am I to understand that she hadn't told you either?'

'Yes, that would be correct.'

He put his glass down on the table.

'Maybe she didn't know.'

'She knew all right. Now Dr Keane, if you would be so kind, I am a very busy man . . .'

'Of course. I merely came to give you my sympathy. I won't trouble you . . .'

He bowed and left the room.

As he shut the door behind him I was hit by a tumult of anger. Buffeted, blow after blow, to my head, my heart, my guts, my whole body was shaken by the blows.

Bitch. The word burst out of my mouth. Bitch. So many years since I had touched her body. So many years. Who?

I ran into the drawing room and slammed the door behind me. I slammed down the open lid of the piano – her piano. Who?

I threw her music on the floor, scattering it like leaves in a storm. Lying bitch. I sat down in the big armchair and rested my head against the back. I sat there shaking with my eyes shut and listened as the doctor revved his engine and drove off and there was only silence left. Dark silence.

I have never experienced in my life such a paroxysm of anger, nor had I thought it would be possible for someone like myself to behave in such a way. Even now, so many hours later, I can feel the remnants of the storm disturbing me. What is the point in my asking myself all the questions that are in my head? I will never be able to answer them. Who was he, this invader of my privacy? What man did she know? I never heard her mention one; among all those Annabelles, Marie-Louises and Shirls there was no mention of a man. Would Josie know? Would she have confided in her? Dare I cross-examine Josie? Perhaps letting this secret out into the world? No. It will be my secret. I will not let this secret out into the world; like Juliet and the boy it will be buried deep.

She was not Juliet, nor Jude, but Judas.

He had underlined the last words with a thick black line.

She imagined him sitting at his desk, his fine hands stretched out in front of him, his two heavy gold rings glinting in the evening light. Still as a statue in her mind's eye until, all of a sudden, he slapped the book shut and thrust it into a drawer of his desk, as if he never wanted to see it again.

Annie felt the same. She didn't want to see again that thick black line or those words he had written. *She was not Juliet, nor Jude, but Judas.*

Such an epitaph.

Such an ending for her beautiful mother.

'I am dying, Egypt, dying.' The words were whispered quite clearly.

Annie got up and crossed the room to where her suitcase sat by the wall. She picked it up and threw it fiercely on to the bed.

'Leave me alone,' she shouted. She opened the lid of the case and began to throw her belongings willy nilly into it.

The telephone rang and for a moment she wondered whether or not to answer it.

'Yes?' Her voice sounded querulous.

'I just wondered where you were. It's after quarter to eight and I'm waiting downstairs.'

Kevin.

She had forgotten about Kevin.

She glanced at herself in the glass on the back of the wardrobe door. She looked raving mad.

'Annie?'

Her eyes were red, her hair like Medusa.

'Annie. Are you all right?'

'Umm. Yes. Give me ten minutes. Have a drink. Order me a large brandy. Ten minutes. Book a table for dinner. I don't want to go out, it's going to rain. Yes. Yes, yes. I'll be down in ten minutes.'

'Are you all right?'

She slammed down the receiver. She searched in her case for her hairbrush, raked with her fingers through the mess in there; no sign. She got up and moved in a distracted way through the room. I don't want to have dinner with him, she thought. Do not want. Imagine, I might have fallen for this man, this Kevin man, this lover of my mother. Ah, there it is, hiding behind the toothpaste.

She began to brush her hair.

This . . . this lying toad. Deceiver. Her hair splayed out around her head, filled with electricity, filled with anger. Deceiver. She threw the brush down on the table. He was lovable; she felt that about him but she couldn't find that in him any longer, that lovable streak. Monstrous liar, more like. Why should she go downstairs and have dinner with him? Why should she listen to any more of his tales? But she would. She would be icy with him, icy. That was the way to be. She picked up the brush once more and calmly smoothed her hair, then searched for the last of the diaries and put it into her pocket. She stood up and looked at herself in the mirror. Grimmish, she thought, but it's the way I am. I'll do.

'I'll do,' she said aloud and left the room, slamming the door behind her.

Kevin was sitting at a table near the door of the bar. The glass by his hand was half full of black liquid and on the other side of the table stood her double brandy. She put one hand into her pocket and clutched at the diary and with the other hand she picked up the brandy and took a good swig.

'Thanks.' She put the glass on the table again and stood looking down at him. He didn't quite know what to do. Stand up? Stay seated? Which was she expecting?

'Will you sit down?' He gestured at the chair across the table. She paid no heed. She just stood there, staring at him. He got up and moved towards her. 'Annie?' He put his hand on her shoulder, but she shook it off. 'I thought we were friends,' he said quietly. She took the diary from her pocket and placed it carefully on the table.

'I think you should read this before . . . before we have dinner . . .' she pushed the book towards him with her fingers stretched straight in front of her, '. . . before we make any comments about being friends.'

He looked down at the book and his face went white; he looked up towards her and she was gone, vanished into thin air. He pulled the book towards him and flipped through empty page after empty page.

This is all. This is the end. I will write no more.

Black.

He shut the little book and pushed it away across the table.

'No,' he said aloud. 'I will not.' But why not? asked a voice in his head. She has read it. Maybe you will learn something.

Unlikely. What could that man teach me?

He felt a little hiccup of sorrow coming up his throat. I can't sit here and bawl. He took a drink of Guinness. Must not sit here and bawl. Must not bawl.

She wants me to read it. What have I to lose?

He put out his hand and drew the little black book across the table. His fingers trembled as he turned the pages.

This is all. This is the end. I will write no more.

He read very slowly. His fingers trembled as he turned the pages. When he came to the last underlined words he put his head in his hands and began to cry.

Annie wasn't far away. There was a group of three armchairs in a corner of the hall, just beyond the reception desk; she had slipped way down into one of them and hoped that she had become invisible. She held the glass of brandy in one hand and sipped at it from time to time, and from time to time the glass rattled against her teeth. She leaned forward to put the glass down on the table and she saw his shadow on the polished wood. He stood there, his face streaked with the tears that had cascaded from his eyes a few minutes before.

'Are you coming to have dinner?' he asked.

'No.'

'Why not?'

'Why not? What do you mean why not? Haven't you told me lies and lies and . . . I don't want to hear any more.'

'I told you what I thought to be the truth.'

'You told me that she had had an abortion. That you had helped her to do it.'

'I thought she had. It never occurred to me to think

anything else. I believed what she told me. Every bloody word she told me.'

She felt in her pocket and pulled out a bundle of tissues. 'Here. Your face is a mess. Mop it up.'

He took the tissues and blotted at his cheeks. It didn't seem to do much good. 'Is that OK now?'

'No. You'd better go and wash it. You look a fright.'

He bowed his head submissively and turned to go. 'Clean face. Then dinner.' The words came back to her over his shoulder.

'Oh, for God's sake. OK.'

When he came back from the Gents with his face clean and shining she was sitting in the same chair, her body crunched forward over a new glass of brandy. She looked as if she could have done with a wash too, he thought. He wondered how things would have been if he had summoned Aunt to his aid when the whole thing started to fall apart. Sure, she would have shouted at him, scolded him, but she would have been on his side and Jude's side. She would have known what to do, what to say and, very important, to whom she should say it.

He put the diary down on the table beside her glass.

'I don't want it. You can have it. You can have them all. They're up in my room. We can fetch them before you go.'

'I don't want them either. I couldn't bear to have them in the house. I couldn't bear the weight of them. Come on, let's go and eat and talk. We have to talk. That's most important.'

She shook her head. 'I want to stay here. I don't want to go into the dining room. I like it better here. It's dark. I don't want to be in the light. They can bring us sandwiches and a bottle of wine. That would suit me best. Please, Kevin.'

He nodded and disappeared into the darkness.

She could hear his voice murmuring to the woman behind the reception desk; she wondered what they would say to each other when he came back. He would yatter and she would keep silent. Yes. That would be best, to keep silent, to reverence the brother she had found and lost in such a brief space of time. Silence is reverence, she thought, and my silence will be for ever as Jude would have wished as she took them both into silence, the child wrapped safely inside her body.

She looked up and saw him standing on the other side of the table and forced herself to smile at him. 'Sit down.'

'They'll bring us sandwiches in a while, and some wine.' He pulled a chair round beside her and sat. 'I know how you feel,' he said. 'I understand the rage and torment that must be in you, but please, please, you must believe that I didn't know. These last few days I have only spoken the truth to you.'

Silence.

'Do you believe me?'

She shrugged her shoulders. 'I don't know.'

'Well, you must. You might at least try.'

'We seem to find it so easy to tell lies. I don't mean just you, not just the people I know, but everyone here. It's like an infectious disease. I sound like a prig, but I'm not. I promise you I'm not. I've just lost a brother I didn't know I ever had. I feel full of shock. And Jude . . . my mother . . . it's such a horrible story. I wanted to come back here and find happiness.'

He laughed.

'Why are you laughing?'

'You don't find happiness, you make it. You make it sound like an Easter egg hunt. Lift a stone and there it is sparkling at you. Yoo hoo, I'm happiness.'

'Oh, do shut up.'

'Look, Annie, I know this has all been a shock to you, it has to me too, but it's the past: over, done with.'

She shook her head. 'It's not the past to me.'

'Well it should be. Your mother, my Jude, was a precious creature and she should still be alive and the baby should be a man now, and in a fairy story we'd all be happy, but who is to say what is right and what is wrong in our story, who is to blame and who is not to blame? Certainly no blame can be cast in your direction, that's for sure.'

The waitress's shoes creaked as she came across the hall with a tray. Kevin and Annie fell silent. The girl put a bottle of red wine down on their table, with two glasses, a plate of sandwiches, a couple of napkins.

'Anything else?' she asked.

'No thank you. That's fine. If we need anything I'll whistle.'

A smile crossed her face. 'You might get me sacked if you do.'

'I'll not risk it so.'

She creaked away again. Kevin picked up the bottle and poured them each a glass of wine. He pushed one over towards Annie. 'Here.' He held his own one up. 'To our memories of Jude.'

She lay back in her chair and looked at him. 'No,' she said. 'I'd rather not.'

He sighed and then took a sip from his glass. 'Right you be. You know, she just wanted safety, not just for herself but for the people she loved most, you, me, and this little baby, and I think that she thought that what she was going to do would ensure that we would be safe, and your father too. He wouldn't know what she had done to him, and the little baby would feel no pain, he would just go safely with her. She would mind him to the end, his eyes still shut.'

Silence.

'You must remember her as a good, fragile person. She was dogged by ill luck. I suppose I was part of that. I don't know. I really don't know. I hate the feeling that I was part of someone's ill luck. One thing I'm sure of is that we would have been happy together.'

'Maybe you would.' Her voice sounded as if she didn't believe him. 'Then again, maybe you wouldn't. Why do things disintegrate the way they do? Everything seems to disintegrate. Perhaps she was right, and death is the better option.'

He laughed. He took a slurp from his glass. 'Have a drink, Miss Gloomy. Tomorrow we'll go and have a good look at your shop and you'll feel much better. The sun will shine, and we'll take Aunt out to dinner. You will realise that life is not too bad after all. Go on, it's nice wine, have a sip.'

'Tomorrow,' she said, picking up her glass and raising it, 'I am going.' She drank.

'Going where?'

'Back to London. Home.' She drank again. 'I don't know why I ever thought that this would be the place for me. It's too full of ghosts and memories and horrible tales that I don't want to hear.' She gave a little laugh. 'I don't like the east wind in London, but apart from that it's an OK place to lead your life.'

'What about your bookshop?'

'For the time being, anyway, I'll go back to the Johns, if they'll have me, and we'll see how things work out. It will all be just as if nothing had ever happened, only this time round I'll have some money. Like the queen. I'll be in the parlour eating bread and honey. Very good, expensive honey. Like the queen. Perhaps, perhaps. I might buy myself a little cottage in the west, Clare, somewhere like that, with sea air and the wonderful smell that mountains have. I'd like to do that. I suppose it all depends on how much the house will bring. Maybe nobody will want to buy it, and then I will let it gradually fall down. It will become a noble ruin, like so many others in this country, probably more noble than their owners ever were. Ha ha. "We are no petty people." Who says, Mr Yeats? We're as petty as the rest of them, turning the quick buck, telling our charming lies, singing our sad songs, pulling the wool – we pull a lot of wool. Yes. If I stayed here I could see myself becoming a wool puller of the highest order.'

She stood up and raised her glass towards him and then tossed the remainder of the liquid in it down her throat.

'Ta-ra,' she said. 'Give my regards to your aunt. Thank her for offering to show me the picture, but I'm not really sorry I didn't see it. My life starts tomorrow. That picture is part of a past that I really wish to leave behind. I don't suppose I'll be seeing you again, so ta-ra. Tararaboomdeay.'

She turned and walked bravely towards the staircase. She left him sitting there with the wine and the sandwiches with nothing to do but listen to her footsteps as she climbed the stairs.

BEHIND THE SCENES AT TINDER PRESS . . .